THE ITALIAN
DEMANDS
HIS HEIRS

LYNNE GRAHAM

MILLS & BOON

First Published in Great Britain 2019
by Mills & Boon, an imprint of HarperCollins*Publishers*
1 London Bridge Street, London, SE1 9GF

© 2019 Lynne Graham

ISBN: 978-0-263-27047-1

MIX
Paper from
responsible sources
FSC® C007454

This book is produced from independently certified FSC™ paper
to ensure responsible forest management.
For more information visit www.harpercollins.co.uk/green.

Printed and bound in Spain
by CPI, Barcelona

CHAPTER ONE

STAMBOULAS FOTAKIS WAS in a grim mood as he surveyed the dossier sited squarely in front of him on his desk. To the side of it sat the much thinner file containing an investigative report on his quarry, Raffaele di Mancini.

Raffaele di Mancini, his granddaughter Vivi's bête noire, the man who had wronged her without reason.

Another good-looking bastard, he thought irritably, flipping the folder open to scan his victim's perfectly chiselled profile, which would have done justice to any male supermodel. Obviously, his three granddaughters liked handsome men. Well, he had settled his eldest granddaughter Winnie's problems, even if that hadn't quite turned out as he had planned when she had elected to stay married to the father of her son.

Vivi, however…bright, hot-tempered Vivi…would be a much tougher nut to crack than the more biddable Winnie. He had had a huge argument with Vivi at his seventy-fifth birthday party, something of a novelty for a man who generally only met with fear and flattery. Being very rich and very influential, Stam was more accustomed to those who did exactly as he told them to do. But not Vivi, he reminisced fondly, Vivi who had no fear of him and spoke her mind without hesitation and, surprisingly, he respected her the more for her inner strength and conviction.

Fortunately for him, however, Vivi utterly loathed Raffaele di Mancini for the way he had wrecked her life. Two years earlier he had ruined her reputation to ensure that his flighty little sister came out of the same scandal whiter than white. Vivi had been accused, not only of being a prostitute, but also of having lured Arianna into stripping off for the camera and signing up as an escort with a sleazy business masquerading as a legitimate modelling agency. No, there was little chance of Vivi falling in love with Mancini, Stam conceded with an amused smile. But of the three potential husbands he had originally lined up to rescue his granddaughters' reputations, Raffaele di Mancini was undeniably the most dangerous as well as being the biggest mystery.

Raffaele, billionaire banker and noted philanthropist, was the descendant of an extravagantly long and blue-blooded family line that could trace its beginnings back to the tenth century. By repute, he was a genius in the financial field and he led a remarkably discreet and conservative life, never ever seeking publicity. That made it all the harder for Stam to understand why Mancini had broken the discretion of a lifetime and labelled poor Vivi an escort on the back of the slenderest evidence. Had he somehow imagined it would shield his kid sister, Arianna, from being associated with the sleazy operation both young women had innocently become embroiled with?

But what did that matter now when the damage had been done? Stam ruminated. His problem was that Mancini was too clever by far to be entrapped by the usual ploys and too rich and virtuous to be bribed. That had meant that Stam was forced to stoop to a means of persuasion that he disliked intensely, particularly when that file revealed that Mancini had spent his adult life struggling to protect his wayward sister from her mistakes and their consequences. It was commendable that he had gone to so much trouble for a girl who was only a half-sister and the daughter of the drug-addled stepmother he could only have despised.

Mancini, however, deserved everything he had coming to him for what he had done to poor Vivi's self-esteem, Stam reflected with harsh finality.

Raffaele di Mancini was uneasy.

And he didn't know why, which nagged at him because he always trusted his gut. Yet there was nothing wrong in his world. His life ran with machine-like efficiency from the instant he arose at six in the morning to a perfectly cooked breakfast to the moment he retired to a bed made up with the very finest bed linen available.

All was quiet within his family circle as well. His younger sister, Arianna, for a long time a source of concern, was finally settled and on the brink of marrying a suitable man, with whom she was currently sharing a home in Florence. He had neither worries nor any thorny problems to tackle.

In London to speak at a banking conference, he had been surprised to be invited to a meeting with the notoriously reclusive Stamboulas Fotakis at his palatial and multi-storeyed London apartment. Fotakis was one of the richest men in the world but Raffaele had never met him and naturally he was curious to discover what had prompted such an invitation. He was also curious about the man himself, he acknowledged wryly. Over the years, reams had been written about Stam Fotakis and even if half of the stories could be discounted as nonsense, what remained was the stuff of legend.

Raffaele raked impatient fingers through his cropped black hair and checked his designer watch. Being kept waiting was a new experience for him. Raised to believe that good manners were integral to good business practice, Raffaele frowned, dark-as-charcoal eyes flaring with irritation. Clearly, Fotakis was running late but Raffaele was keen to get back to his town house and unwind after a very long day spent answering stupid questions and being sociable. Raffaele had a very low tolerance threshold for fools. Labelled a genius at school, he was impatient, extremely organised and only happy when following a precise schedule.

A PA, a beautiful blonde, entered the reception room and ushered him into a lift, where she tried to strike up a conversation and flirt with him. Stiffening in exasperation at her hair-tossing, fluttering eyelashes and lingering glances, Raffaele behaved much like a man swatting off a fly. Women came on to him all the time and it often irritated him. It got in the way of normal dialogue and tainted the professional atmosphere of an office environment. If she had been working for Raffaele, he would have instantly sacked her for such a display.

Women had their place in his life, of course they did. Raffaele had a high sex drive, as with many other thirty-year-old men. But he was infinitely more discreet than most. He chose his lovers with care and none of his affairs lasted longer than a few weeks. There was even a good reason for that brief timescale. Raffaele had eventually worked out that the longer he spent with a woman, the more attached and ambitious and indiscreet she became. As he had no intention of getting married until he was in his forties and mature enough to make a wise choice, he enjoyed sex only as long as it came without strings.

Raffaele was shown into a wood-panelled office of almost Victorian magnificence. Another door opened and a small white-haired, bearded man appeared. He immediately lifted the fat file on the desk and extended it to Raffaele. 'Mr di Mancini,' Stam Fotakis murmured flatly.

'Mr Fotakis.' Somewhat disconcerted by the lack of social chit-chat even though he had very little time for such time-wasting pursuits, Raffaele accepted the file and took the seat his host indicated.

'Give me your thoughts on that,' Stam invited smoothly.

As Raffaele leafed ever more slowly through the incredibly detailed file with a rare sense of growing horror, he breathed in slow and deep to steady himself. Arianna's every mistake seemed to be included in that file and there were one or two that not even Raffaele had known about. He swallowed hard on his shock at being presented with such a shady dossier on his little sister's past activities.

'What are you planning to do with this information?' Raffaele enquired in as civil a tone as he could manage because he was angry, seriously angry, and that was an emotion he rarely experienced but instinctively knew had to be controlled.

His host surveyed him steadily. 'That very much depends on you. It will be released to the tabloid press only if you disappoint me,' he revealed quietly.

'That is an unthinkable threat,' Raffaele breathed tautly. 'I cannot believe that my sister has ever done you any harm.'

'Let me explain the connection,' Stam urged him stonily. 'It's the tale of two young women, one born into rank and privilege and great wealth…your sister.'

'And the other?' Raffaele prompted impatiently.

'Born into poor circumstances and raised without any advantages but nonetheless a hard-working, educated and respectable young woman…and *my* granddaughter.'

'Your granddaughter,' Raffaele repeated blankly, still trying to fathom at top speed what Stam Fotakis could possibly want from him to warrant such a threat.

'Vivien Mardas, better known as Vivi,' Stam supplied. 'For a little while she was a friend of your sister's.'

Raffaele went rigid, the link established and comprehension now possible. 'I remember her,' he said stiffly. 'She is a member of your family?'

'Yes,' Stam said, equally stiffly. 'And I am as protective of her as you are of your sister and determined to rectify any injustices she has suffered.'

Raffaele remained diplomatically silent, for a slow,

deep anger was burning like hellfire inside him as he joined the dots and hit pay dirt. When he had known her, Vivi had definitely been unaware that she had a very rich and powerful grandfather. Evidently, having discovered that no doubt welcome reality, she had lied about the less presentable parts of her past in an effort to cover them up.

'Injustices?' he prompted flatly.

'You ruined her reputation by referring to her as a prostitute. As that ludicrous designation and the story is still available online to anyone who cares to look her up, Vivi found it impossible to find a job commensurate with her abilities,' Stam revealed. 'She suffered a great deal for someone who was innocent of fault. Her friends dropped her, her name was bandied about. She was laughed at, despised and she was obliged to leave jobs until she was finally forced to legally take another surname to hide that embarrassing past. She is now known as Vivien Fox.'

Raffaele nodded, that little sob story of Vivi's woes touching him not at all. Of course, he wasn't an elderly man, keen to believe only the best of his grandchild, he reasoned without hesitation. He was cool, logical, innately critical and suspicious, particularly when it came to labelling a woman an innocent. He had yet to meet a genuinely innocent woman.

He remembered Vivi *very* well. Hair that glittered like copper wire in the sunlight but which felt like spun silk. A tall, beautiful redhead, who could look impossibly elegant in anything she wore, even jeans. Skin like translucent porcelain and eyes as brilliant a blue as the

Italian summer sky. He also remembered how *very* close he had come to succumbing to her wiles, even though she didn't fit his preferred expectations of a woman in any field. He had had a narrow escape there and he was still grateful for it and not one bit regretful for anything he had said that could have offended Stam Fotakis.

Unless his misfortune in offending Stam was to lead to his kid sister being harmed, he adjusted grudgingly. And harmed Arianna very definitely would be, if that dossier of her past foolishness was ever to be released to the press, because her fiancé's family were very conventional, and he would come under a lot of pressure to ditch her. That would send Arianna reeling and straight back into the erratic behaviour she had left behind her after falling in love with Tomas.

'I don't know what you want from me,' Raffaele intoned levelly. 'But I cannot believe that you genuinely want to injure another naive young woman like my sister. Arianna was born with problems.'

Stam lifted a silencing hand. 'I know she was born addicted to drugs and suffers from poor impulse control. I know she's not particularly bright and is far too trusting of strangers, but she's not my responsibility, she's yours,' he pointed out calmly. 'To make restitution, I want you to marry Vivi and give her your illustrious name.'

'*Marry* her?' Raffaele exclaimed in angry disbelief before he clenched his jaw shut and bit back any unwise comments as to the likelihood of Vivi's much-vaunted innocence.

'Only for the ceremony, suitably publicised to give

her proper standing in society,' Stam continued in the same mild tone, much as though he were discussing the weather. 'I want nothing more. You will part on your wedding day and a divorce will duly follow. No financial settlement will be required on her behalf either. It is a modest request.'

'Modest?' Raffaele queried with incredulous emphasis.

'Yes. I have no doubt that you think yourself very much above my granddaughter in terms of background and breeding,' Stam conceded drily. 'I won't hold that against you. But you should be grateful that the temporary use of your good name is all that I require from you in return for that dossier, which would have a catastrophic effect on your sister's marital plans.'

Fotakis knew it *all*, Raffaele acknowledged grittily, and, no matter how outrageous Stam's demand that he marry Vivi, he knew he would have to consider it to protect Arianna's future stability and security. Tomas was charmed by his sister's giggly immaturity and impulsiveness where many men would have run a mile, and he didn't want her only because she was an heiress either. Tomas, as sensible and stable as Arianna was not, was his sister's perfect match and, what was more, Arianna *loved* him.

How could he stand by in silence while she lost all that over matters as trivial as a naked bathing episode in a famous fountain and being mistakenly arrested as a shoplifter? Unhappily, there were other murkier episodes involved and included in that file, he conceded grudgingly, such as the time she had spent the night with two men because her so-called friends had dared her to do so.

'I hated it,' she had muttered guiltily, appalled that he had picked up on that unsavoury rumour. 'But everyone clse had done stuff like that and I wanted to fit in… I wanted them to *like* me.'

After that affair, Raffaele had begun vetting her friends as well, recognising that his sister was too vulnerable to be left at the mercy of those ready to take advantage of her gullible nature to entertain themselves at her expense.

'Presumably you have already discussed this idea with Vivi,' Raffaele remarked curtly. 'And she, of course, will be keen.'

'*Keen?*' Stam surprised him by laughing out loud. 'Vivi hates you and she definitely doesn't want to marry you! I'm afraid that persuading Vivi to the altar is *your* personal challenge.'

'You're seriously expecting me to believe that she isn't involved in this proposition?' Raffaele incised in disbelief.

'Of course, she isn't involved. Vivi doesn't work off logic, she works off emotion. My…er…suggestion that she marry you made her very angry but I'm sure a high achiever of your calibre will know exactly how to transform her view of you,' Stam completed with wry amusement brightening his snapping dark eyes. 'If you want that dossier to stay private, you *have* to get Vivi to the church.'

'That's to be my penance, is it?' Raffaele pronounced between gritted teeth.

'If you like to think of it in those terms, do so. It's immaterial to me. You give her a wedding ring but you keep your hands off her,' Stam Fotakis warned him bluntly. 'I want her back as untouched and unharmed as she is now. Is that understood?'

Dark colour edged the smooth planes of Raffaele's high cheekbones, accentuating his taut bone structure. He could not credit the warning he was being given. 'I have never touched an unwilling woman in my life,' he countered with icy hauteur.

'Well, you will find my granddaughter very unwilling,' Stam forecast with satisfaction. 'I dare say you're accustomed to a different response from women…although you didn't rise to the bait of my PA giving you a come-on in the lift.'

'That was a set-up?' Raffaele breathed in thundering disbelief, momentarily betrayed into speech.

'I like to know the nature of the men I deal with and you passed the test. You're not a womaniser,' Stam retorted crisply. 'I am very protective of Vivi.'

It was on the tip of Raffaele's tongue to say that on the one occasion he had had Vivi in his arms, the very last thing she had been was unwilling, but he swallowed back that unwise admission, choosing instead to be grateful that there were, after all, *some* things that Vivi's grandfather did *not* know.

And now, Raffaele reflected as he travelled back to his London town house in the comfort of his limo, he had to decide what to do next. It was ironic that he had always had the comfortable belief that being very, very rich protected you, he conceded, stunned into shock and an unfamiliar sense of powerlessness by the situation he found himself in. But wealth hadn't, after all, protected Arianna from her misfortunes from conception, nor was it sufficient to hold at bay an old man determined to claim restitution for a sin that Raffaele had not actually committed.

He had *not* called Vivi a prostitute. For a start, she had been an escort rather than a prostitute and he knew the difference, having met women of both persuasions in even the most exclusive circles and learned how to detect and avoid them. That Vivi had almost slipped past his guard still infuriated him. The prostitution designation, however, had been manufactured by the press to provide an attention-grabbing headline.

Unfortunately, that truth would not remove that dangerous dossier on his sister from Stam Fotakis's calculating and vengeful hands...

An upsetting memory was playing through Vivi's mind as she put on her make-up for her date with her boyfriend, Jude. She had had a blazing row with her grandfather during his birthday party at her sister and brother-in-law's home in Greece and she hadn't let off steam by telling her sisters about it because she had known it would upset them when they preferred to play happy families.

'Once Mancini marries you, you will never have cause to fear that scandal again because naturally the man who referred to you in those terms would scarcely be marrying you if you *were* a...er...woman of ill repute.' Her grandfather selected the phrase with distaste.

'Obviously, a rich, extremely successful man from his aristocratic background would never consider such a wife.'

'I'd sooner marry a toad than Raffaele di Mancini!' Vivi flung back at the older man in furious disbelief. 'But the real truth is that I don't want to marry *anyone*!'

'Winnie is happy,' he reminded her doggedly.

'My sister's a people pleaser and I'm not!' Vivi countered with spirit. 'I love her to death but what's all right for her isn't all right for me. When I get married, I want it to be *real*, not some phoney cobbled-together arrangement for the sake of appearances and status!'

'I can't believe you'd want to *keep* Mancini!' Stam sniped, refusing to get the point or listen and hanging onto his mindset with the tenacity of a bulldog gnawing at a particularly tough bone.

Refusing to rise to that bait, Vivi tossed her head. 'I can't believe you're such a miser that you couldn't save my foster parents' home for them without attaching unreasonable conditions to your generosity! We're supposed to be family but you don't behave like family are supposed to behave. But then what would I know about that, never really having had that experience?' she muttered, falling into an awkward silence.

'You are my family and I will *always* look after you,' Stam intoned stubbornly.

'Looking after me is not marrying me off…however briefly…to that Mancini rat! And how could you possibly persuade him to marry me anyway?' she demanded suspiciously. 'I suspect he would sooner go to his grave than agree to marry a woman he believes to have been a prostitute.'

In his old-fashioned way, Stam winced and sighed, 'I have what you could call an irresistible proposition to lay before Mancini, which will persuade him.'

'I don't care if you're offering him the moon as an inducement. Well, actually I *do*,' Vivi admitted on a fresh gust of anger that made her almost violet eyes shimmer as bright as polar stars against her porcelain skin. 'Having anything to do with him at all, never mind marrying him, would be humiliating!'

'No,' Stam had argued equally strongly. 'This time around, all the power will be in *your* hands, Vivi. Don't you want that experience? Don't you want to see the man who insulted you forced to eat his own words?'

No, Vivi could live without revenge, she conceded as she emerged from the memory of that argument. As long as she never saw Raffaele di Mancini again in this lifetime, she would be happy. He was a reminder of too much that she wanted to forget and leave buried. She had become very fond of Arianna and, no doubt at Raffaele's behest, Arianna had immediately dumped their friendship as well. And then there had been her seemingly growing relationship with Raffaele himself at the time. She closed off that train of thought angrily. Just a stupid kiss, just *one* stupid kiss, even a teenager would have known not to get unduly excited by some- thing that trivial, she castigated herself.

But then Vivi knew that she tended to be more vul- nerable with men than other more experienced and emo- tionally secure women. Vivi had not known security until she was fourteen and living with her final set of foster parents, the kindly John and Liz, who had re-united the three sisters within their home. Before John and Liz, there had been a series of unsuitable foster homes where Vivi had been bullied, verbally abused and, on several occasions, sexually threatened.

Winnie, Vivi and Zoe had lost their parents in a car accident. At the age of twenty-three, Vivi barely re-membered them. Their father, however, had been Stam's youngest son, who had been estranged from him for years. Stam had not even known his grandchildren ex-isted until they had contacted him as adults, seeking his financial help when their foster parents were facing the repossession of their home where they were still caring for troubled children. He had welcomed them into his life with great enthusiasm but had set outrageous terms for giving them his help, demanding that they all marry men of his choice to raise their status.

Vivi had still to make up her mind about what she thought of her grandfather. Was he, simply, an incred-ible snob? Or crazy? Or, more worryingly, the kind of personality who had to get revenge on anyone who wronged a member of his family? Well, Winnie and Vivi had been wronged but their youngest sister, Zoe, had only been wronged by unfortunate foster care. Vivi knew she had to stand up to her grandfather for Zoe's sake because Zoe was frail and emotionally vulnera-ble, subject to extreme shyness and panic attacks. Zoe would never manage to fight with the older man; in-deed Zoe was so self-effacing that the very idea of her confronting anyone struck the bolder Vivi as ridiculous.

For that reason, Vivi knew that *she* had to stand strong. She tried not to be bitter about the past, for bitterness achieved nothing. At present she and Zoe were living in a small, luxurious town house owned by their grandfather and offered to them rent-free. But the house felt empty without Winnie's toddler son, Teddy, running about and Vivi was too distrustful of her grandfather to spend the money she wasn't currently forking out on rent. Instead she was saving that money, waiting anxiously for the day when he might tire of her defiance and throw them back out into the cold.

That meant that she still couldn't afford to get her awful hair straightened again, she thought ruefully, picking up a corkscrew copper curl and dropping it again with antipathy. It was the hair from hell and she had been born with it and she was only content with her appearance when she could transform it into a smooth straight fall. Right now it was rioting across her shoulders, round her face and down her back like a rag doll's wig, she thought irritably. Not that Jude, her current boyfriend, seemed to mind.

But then Jude didn't really seem to mind much about anything. She had met him at her gym where he worked as a martial arts teacher. He was blond and laid-back, and he had a good body but she had yet to experience a desire to see that body naked. Possibly their casual relationship came down to being mates more than anything else, she reflected ruefully. If she hadn't met Raffaele and been immediately attracted to him, she would've believed that she was really not that bothered about sex. Men usually came and went in Vivi's life without her ever particularly caring. Only Raffaele had hurt her and that had come along with a whole lot of other damage so she tried not to dwell on his rejection.

It was thanks to Raffaele that she had been forced to work in a succession of menial jobs before finally surrendering to the very effective changing of her surname. Only then had she contrived to shed the scandal that had seen her hounded out of two good jobs. And all because she had taken a first job straight after graduating with her marketing degree as a receptionist in a business that had ultimately turned out to be functioning as a modelling *and* an undercover escort agency, with many of the models working as escorts on the side. And as if that hadn't proved bad enough a pop-up brothel had been operating in the back of the building as well, and it had been the police raid of that facility that had exploded the agency's cover and led to her being captured on camera running down the street to escape the whole explosive mess. That photo and her name had been splashed over a notorious tabloid newspaper and in that photo she had looked ridiculously glamorous, because Arianna had cleared out her wardrobe and had given her a pile of her discarded but still gorgeous outfits to wear.

Her phone buzzed and she lifted it, hoping it wasn't Jude calling to cancel because she had been looking forward to the film they were supposed to be seeing. Instead a voice she had hoped never to hear again sounded in her ears. That voice was deep and rich and accented with a positive purr. Even Raffaele's voice dripped sex appeal, she had once thought, but right at that moment, with the phone clamped too tightly to her ear, she couldn't think rationally at all because that he should actually *dare* to contact her had not only never occurred to her but it also plunged her deep into shock.

'Vivi?' he queried. 'It's Raffaele. We need to talk.'

Vivi rang off without speaking and immediately blocked his number. He might be willing to dance to her grandfather's tune for the right price but she was not. Or was she? She thought of John and Liz's predicament and the great debt she and her siblings owed to the couple for their kindness and care at a time when the girls had been young and vulnerable. And then she felt sick with uncertainty while she wondered how Raffaele had got her phone number. *We need to talk.* Raffaele di Mancini, born into an Italian dukedom even if he didn't use his title, just had to be kidding! Only if he had a sense of humour he had never revealed it to her.

He was good at staring though, she recalled abstractedly, suddenly thrown back to their first meeting over the meal that Arianna had insisted on inviting her to. And all Arianna's intimidating brother had seemed to do was stare at her, eyes as dark as jet between thick black lashes. Eyes that were set in an extravagantly handsome face, eyes that could unexpectedly warm to a melted golden caramel hue and send her heartbeat inexplicably racing.

Yes, there had been very little normal getting-to-know-you conversation over that family dinner with poor Arianna being left to pick up the slack and usually sharp Vivi finding her tongue inexplicably glued to the roof of her mouth for the first time in her life.

And what had she done? While Arianna had blithely chattered, Vivi had stared back, fascinated by Raffaele in the strangest way, little arrows of heat darting through her as she'd noticed new and seemingly important things about him. The commanding angle of his black brows; the masculine strength of his jaw line; the olive-toned planes and hollows of his fabulous bone structure; the classic arch of his nose and the wildly sensual curve of his sculpted lips. She had noted his perfect manners, his elegant hands and the fluid movement of them. She had sat there like a schoolgirl ogling him, forgetting to eat, forgetting everything, seduced by the new energising excitement filtering through her bloodstream like a charge of adrenalin.

And much good it had done her, she recollected with self-loathing, emerging back into the less exciting present…

Across London, Raffaele cast down his phone and moved without hesitation on to Plan B. Vivi wouldn't speak to him. Well, he had to admit that that was a surprise but he *had* to find a way to make her deal with him. If civil and calm didn't work as an approach, he would take a leaf out of her grandfather's book and try heavy duty persuasion. And if that didn't work out either, he would work right through the alphabet in plans until he found the magic combination to *make* Vivi do what he needed her to do for Arianna's benefit.

Raffaele had a rare sleepless night, spent remembering his dismay at his stepmother's sudden death from an overdose when he was only twenty and still a student. Her passing, mere months after his father's demise, had impacted heavily on Raffaele's life. Without any warning or preparation, he had found himself responsible for a twelve-year-old girl, a twelve-year-old girl he had barely bothered to even get to know…his half-sister. Yet he had grown to love Arianna and care for her in a way he had never deemed possible, for he knew his own flaws and accepted that he was essentially cold and analytical in nature.

Lying awake in the dark hours, however, he had discovered that he couldn't suddenly switch off that deep need to protect his vulnerable sister from the drug inheritance that had damaged her through no fault of her own. Arianna harmed herself, never anybody else. So, he would do *whatever* it took to protect her from the fallout of that unfortunate friendship with Vivi two years earlier…and Vivi?

Well, devious, sexy little Vivi was simply going to have to bite the bullet and pay her dues on Arianna's behalf…

CHAPTER TWO

'THE RUMOUR IS that the business has been taken over,' Vivi's manager, Janice, declared nervously. 'Hacketts Tech now belongs to a big consortium and you know what *that* means…don't you?'

Unaccustomed to Janice being anxious, Vivi frowned. 'No, I haven't had that experience before.'

'Well, I have…*twice* before,' the older woman declared ruefully. 'First, the new bosses tell you there're going to be no big changes and then they start restructuring, bringing in their own staff and suddenly you're out of a job!'

Vivi grimaced. 'My goodness, I hope not. I like it here.'

She checked her emails and was surprised to find that she had an appointment at ten with someone from the top floor that she had never heard of. She ran the name against the staff list and couldn't find it. Did that mean that Janice's rumour was true and that the process was already starting? Telling herself not to jump to conclusions, she kept quiet about the email.

'Miss Fox?' The receptionist checked when Vivi arrived at the top floor, leaving her desk to show Vivi where to go.

'Who is this person I'm to see?' Vivi questioned helplessly.

'The new owner of the business. I'm not supposed to mention his name. It's all very hush-hush,' the woman told her apologetically.

Registering that Janice's rumour was true, Vivi raised her brows in silence while wondering why a junior member of the marketing team would qualify for an appointment with the new owner. Some particular query? Then why not call up Janice?

But as the door was knocked on deferentially and duly opened wide, all suddenly became clear as Raffaele di Mancini swung round from the view he had been contemplating from the window of the contemporary office.

'Come in, Vivi,' he instructed cool as ice.

Vivi was frozen with shock on the threshold, her slender body rigid with tension because Raffaele's sudden appearance in her life in an environment where she could not tell him to go jump off a cliff was as disturbing as it was horrifying.

Evidently grasping that reality for himself, Raffaele crossed the room, tugged her over the threshold as if she were a small and hesitant child and closed the door behind her. 'Now let's talk like grown-ups,' he advised, disconcerted by the changes in her.

The smooth swathe of copper hair he recalled had transformed into a gorgeous foaming mane of silky curls, rather like a woman in a pre-Raphaelite portrait, he found himself vaguely acknowledging. Add in the china pale complexion and the bright blue eyes above that full pink mouth and you had a woman whom he might despise, but whose attractions added up to a quite remarkable level of beauty. Of course, he had noticed that she was stunning before, that being a fact that no man would fail to note, he reasoned, impatient with the way in which his brain was suddenly shooting out random thoughts like a shotgun. There she stood in an undeniably plain straight black skirt and pale blue shirt that still highlighted the perfection of her tall, slender figure with its modest curves. She stood about five feet nine in height and Raffaele had liked that about her because he preferred taller women, being six feet four himself.

'I'm not staying. I refuse to be manipulated like this!' Vivi exclaimed, spinning round to head back to the door.

'You walk out that door now, I start having redundancies listed,' Raffaele informed her, reckoning that he was likely to learn a lot about Vivi Fox—formerly Mardas—and her character in the next few minutes.

White as snow at that unveiled threat, Vivi spun back. 'You can't do that… I mean, just because I don't want to *speak* to you? That would be outrageous!' she protested in disbelief.

'As the new owner of Hacketts Tech, I can be as outrageous as I like. Any regrets that you didn't simply agree to talk to me last night on the phone?' Raffaele elevated an ebony brow, all sardonic and cool, and it made her want to punch him in the gut. 'You see, I don't play games when I'm challenged, I play hardball.'

Vivi was chilled by that warning but she refused to

let *him* see that. 'Like I don't already know that?' she quipped, a fine auburn brow lifting.

'Evidently, you didn't,' Raffaele pointed out while spinning out a chair for her to occupy. 'Now, please take a seat.'

'I prefer to stand, since I'm not planning on staying long,' Vivi asserted, staying where she was, determined to show no weakness.

'Are you normally this contrary?' Raffaele breathed in exasperation, fighting a ridiculous urge to lift her off her feet and simply plonk her down in the designated spot. 'Or is it that you're childish?'

Refusing to look directly at him, Vivi shrugged her unconcern although a faint hint of colour warmed her translucent cheeks. 'You can make your own mind up about that, I'm sure.'

'Why do you think I want to speak to you?'

'Because, apparently, my grandfather has made what he terms an "irresistible proposition" to you in return for which he expects you to marry me…in name only,' Vivi recited with precision.

For a split second, Raffaele toyed with the idea of telling her the truth: that he was being blackmailed. But then what would that mean to her? Why would she care what happened to Arianna, who had not seen her or spoken to her in two years? And even more cogently, did he really want to tell a woman he couldn't trust just how vulnerable his kid sister was? What if she, in a spirit of retaliation, went to the press to expose Arianna's secrets? What if she was just like her rancorous grandfather?

Vivi studied Raffaele closely from beneath her lashes, absolutely hating the fact that her heart was racing so fast it felt as though it were bouncing inside her chest. He unnerved her, he always had, she told herself soothingly. Who could help being intimidated by such a very large and powerful man? But for all that, he was *still* the most beautiful man she had ever seen in her life and even that simple acknowledgement of what was right before her cut through her defences, ensuring that her every muscle went rigid with stress. What was it about him that smashed the composure she had no trouble maintaining with other men?

His cropped hair reflected the light above as dark as the black-as-sloes eyes welded to her in silence. He had perfect symmetrical bone structure, as perfect as a Michelangelo carving in marble. The bronzed tone of his skin, the high cheekbones, the straight nose and the faintly shadowed strong jaw enhancing that wide sensual mouth all played into the same striking effect he had had on her the first time she met him. But she had grown up since then, learned a lot *since then*, she reminded herself with angry urgency, studiously dragging her gaze from him again and choosing to settle down into the chair she had refused only minutes earlier because sitting made it easier not to look at him.

'That "irresistible proposition",' Vivi repeated drily. 'You're rich. You really don't need to be richer unless you've suffered a reverse in circumstances since we last met?'

Incredulous at the tilt of her chin in question, Raffaele gritted his perfect white teeth together because she was making him angry and he didn't 'do' angry with anyone. Angry was out of control, angry was everything that Raffaele always guarded against and restrained and suppressed. 'No, my circumstances are unchanged,' he murmured flatly, struggling to combat the temper she brought out in him with her unstudied insolence.

Nobody spoke to Raffaele with scorn, nobody ever had before and nobody else would have *dared*. His lean brown hands coiled into controlled fists. He could suck it up for Arianna, he told himself urgently, he was *too* proud, it would probably do his character a world of good…but if he ever got the chance for payback he knew he would be grabbing at it with two very greedy hands because Vivi's disrespectful attitude infuriated him.

'You would really be prepared to marry me just to make a profit?' Vivi pressed, finding that so hard to believe.

His dark eyes glittered as though someone had shot them through with diamonds and she blinked, dragging her attention back from him again, disturbed again by his effect on her concentration. 'Why not?' he asked drily.

Vivi clasped her hands together on her lap, in no way as cool as she wanted to be in his presence. He had disconcerted her because she would have sworn he was the last man alive to be seduced merely by money. But then what did she *really* know about Raffaele di Mancini? Hadn't she foolishly believed that she was getting to know him and then been soundly disabused of that belief when he'd turned round and humiliated her,

absolutely humiliated her, by giving way to the unfor-
givable conviction that she was a woman willing to sell
her body for money? She really knew nothing about
Raffaele. He was extremely rich but clearly desired to
be even richer and, if that were the case, it meant that
only she was preventing him from reaching that goal.
And that dismayed her because it meant that both her
grandfather *and* Raffaele were ranged against her as
opponents, which was very much the same as sticking
her between a rock and a hard place.

'I don't want to marry you,' Vivi murmured in a very
quiet voice as she stared at the wall to the left of him.
'I don't want anything to do with you.'

Frustration lanced through Raffaele at finding her as
difficult as her grandfather had forecast. He had been
so sure in his own head that she would snatch at the
opportunity to become his wife, seduced by his social
standing and a need for revenge. Instead she was sitting there in front of him like a stiff little marionette
doll placed in a chair and refusing to react.

Raffaele took a new tack. 'There's nothing inherently
shameful about having been an escort,' he breathed
tautly. 'It's how far you go in that role. If it was merely
companionship you offered, there's nothing wrong with
it.'

'Oh, come on!' Vivi flashed back at him, animation
brightening her formerly still and shuttered face, bright
blue eyes taking on a violet hue as she glanced back at
him less warily than before. 'You know that you don't
really believe that, Raffaele. You believed that I was
flogging my body for money to anyone who offered

sufficient inducement and you acted accordingly and treated me like dirt!' she condemned.

'I did not treat you like dirt,' Raffaele intoned grittily.

'You blamed me for the risky decisions your sister made. I didn't ask her to take off her clothes for that modelling portfolio she was so set on having done!' she argued angrily, wishing that recollection still didn't hurt enough to make her angry. 'She did that all on her own. And when she was approached to do escort work because nobody at the agency knew that she was in-dependently wealthy….how was *that* anything to do with me? I was only the receptionist on the front desk, a humble employee. I didn't know what was going on at that place. I wasn't one of the models doing escort work on the side!'

'So you say,' Raffaele responded between gritted teeth because he didn't believe a word of what she was telling him. A receptionist? Did she think he was stu-pid? A *receptionist* with that beauty and that figure? Of course she had been one of the models and the recep-tionist job had merely been a safe cover story for his benefit, and Arianna's. It was on the tip of his tongue to tell her that the average *humble* receptionist couldn't afford the red-soled shoes she had been captured in print wearing the day the brothel had been raided, but in the circumstances it would be stupid to wind her up more. The newspaper concerned had made much of the very expensive designer apparel she had been wearing, im-plying that she was a *very* exclusive prostitute.

Vivi compressed her lips, totally aware that he didn't believe her. He was such a snob, she thought sourly, so ready to credit nasty stuff about her simply because she had been downright poor in comparison to his sister and himself. What other reason could he have for being so suspicious? It wasn't as if she had acted all alluring with him, was it? Vivi didn't know how, didn't have sufficient experience or the desire to act alluring with any man. She wasn't even very good at flirting because generally the men she met were bolder and cruder than flirting required.

'I'm not going to apologise for the fact that I dislike you,' Vivi fired at him.

'I don't need you to like me to marry me in the kind of paper marriage your grandfather requires,' Raffaele shot back in exasperation.

'Well, there would be nothing in it for me,' Vivi fielded, struggling not to think about her duty in John and Liz's situation of unsettled debts. For yes, there would be something in it for her, she reflected guiltily. In fact, there would be more than one advantage to marrying him. It would help John and Liz, it would please her grandfather and leave her blessedly free to get on with the rest of her life as she saw fit with nobody to please but herself. It would release all her worries *but*... it would also put poor Zoe in the hot seat in her place and how could she allow that?

'If I offered money, diamonds...' Raffaele murmured silkily, seeking her weakness, for he was convinced there had to be one.

'Stop right there!' Vivi cut in angrily. 'How could you bribe me into doing it? My grandfather would give me almost anything I wanted...'

Except the one thing she needed, which was John and Liz's mortgage debt paid off, she completed inwardly.

Resentment darted through her at the reality that her grandfather was holding what was a ridiculously small amount of money on his terms over his granddaughters' heads in an attempt to force them into doing his bidding. Winnie's husband, Eros, might have been trying to find a way of getting around that fact and spiking her grandfather's big guns but he had not, so far, contrived to do so. She needed to phone her sister, though, and check out the latest news on that front.

'Then we would appear to have reached an impasse, for the moment,' Raffaele tacked on because he refused to credit that he wouldn't find a means to achieve her agreement. He never failed at anything he set out to do and saw this situation as no different. Given sufficient time and attention, he would solve the riddle of her reluctance and come up with the magic winning combination. One way or another, he told himself grimly, he would lock her down to protect Arianna.

'We'll have dinner tonight,' he told her flatly.

Vivi tossed her head back, curling ringlets of copper dancing back from her triangular face, bright dark blue eyes defiant. 'No, we won't.'

'Tomorrow night, then.'

The soft full pink lips he couldn't take his eyes off tightened into a surprisingly hard line. 'No.'

'I think you're forgetting about that redundancy list,' Raffaele reminded her silkily, ready to use any weapon he had to force her into doing his bidding.

Vivi leapt out of her chair and called him a very rude

word, colour streaming across her cheekbones, eyes violet-tinged again with sheer fury.

'If not by birth, certainly by nature,' Raffaele countered with hard amusement, thoroughly satisfied to have got a very telling reaction out of her. Temper, temper, he chanted inwardly because she had one hell of a temper.

On the other hand—and who would ever have guessed it? he marvelled—Vivi Fox *cared* about her work colleagues. She wasn't quite the hard-nosed, solely mercenary beauty he had assumed, willing to use anything she had got to better herself in society. Of course, she didn't need to be like that now, he reminded himself impatiently, not with a very rich grandfather behind her.

'I hate you!' she flung at him.

'Dinner at eight tomorrow night. I want you to have time to think over this meeting. A car will pick you up,' Raffaele stated, not batting an eyelash in receipt of her angry attack.

Vivi's fingers turned into claws, biting into her palms. No man had ever filled her with such rage that she felt violent, only him. But she would not run the risk of calling Raffaele's bluff. He was a banker, he was innately ruthless and if redundancies could make her dance to his tune he was unlikely to make an empty threat, she reflected wretchedly. How could she risk that happening? How could she challenge him when her fellow employees' livelihoods could be at stake? For goodness' sake, what on earth had Grandad offered him to make him so desperate to win her agreement?

'Eight.' She bit out the word as if it physically hurt her and in a way it did because giving even an inch to

Raffaele di Mancini felt like a self-betrayal of pride and good judgement.

'I shall look forward to it,' Raffaele dared with purring satisfaction and if there had been anything within reach to throw at him, Vivi would've thrown it.

She went back down to the marketing department in the lift, her brain in a daze after all the emotions she had worked through. Hatred, rage and resentment assailed her in heady waves around Raffaele and it made it hard for her to think straight, to think *smart*, she recognised, finding another stick to beat herself with. If she was cooler, calmer, would she have found a way out? But how could she be cool and calm when he so enraged her?

Her memory went back to the day she had met Arianna with her high heel caught in a grating down the street from the modelling agency. She had only been a week into her first job there and heading out to grab lunch. She had stopped to help Arianna, who was comically trying to drag her shoe out of the grating while standing on one leg like a heron.

'Oh, thanks…' Arianna had said with a flashing friendly smile, a very pretty brunette, who had seemed much the same age as Vivi was.

Nothing had budged that shoe heel from the grating and, wearying of the struggle, Arianna had stepped out of the other one, swept it up, looked at it as if trying to judge what use one shoe would be and then tossed it down again in disgust. Barefoot, she had stepped onto the pavement and introduced herself and Vivi had dug into her capacious tote to offer the use of the shabby trainers she wore to travel into work. Arianna had been as grateful as if she had saved her life and had accompanied Vivi into the café where she was planning to buy a sandwich, confessing that she was hungry herself. And that was how her friendship with Arianna had begun, two young women getting to know each other and exchanging numbers over a snack. Their meeting had not been in any way engineered. Arianna had not been 'targeted' for her wealth, as her brother had implied to the press, because, although Arianna had been very fashionably dressed, Vivi had not recognised the designer style she herself had never been able to afford. She had noticed Arianna's jewellery and had simply assumed it was good costume stuff, rather than the real thing.

Arianna had come into Vivi's life at a time when she was rather lonely. How had she been lonely living with two sisters? Well, back then, Winnie had been heartbroken and pregnant by Eros and no company whatsoever. And love Zoe as Vivi did, Zoe was happier reading a book in her room than in actually going out to meet people. Arianna had been full of life and cheerfulness and Vivi had liked her, felt rather protective of her, too, once she realised that the other young woman was a year younger and seemingly rather naive about city life.

Arianna had confided her dream of becoming a model the evening they had first gone out together, when she had also flashed a gold credit card and taken Vivi to a very exclusive club. That was when a little tactful questioning had revealed that Arianna came from a different world and Vivi had become a little uncomfortable in her company then.

Having spoken to the resident photographer at the

agency, however, Vivi had set up the appointment for Arianna to have a modelling portfolio prepared. The day after, Arianna had invited her to join her and her brother for dinner. Two nights after that, Raffaele had unexpectedly joined them at a club and swept them up to the VIP section, scolding his sister for not being there in the first place. There he had questioned Vivi about her background and occupation and she had said defensively, 'I'm ordinary and I was trying to explain to Arianna that people like you and her don't become best friends with someone like me but she doesn't seem to get that. She just looked hurt.'

'I don't see why you shouldn't be friends,' Raffaele had said, surprising her when she had already decided he *had* to be a snob with his blue-blooded background.

Of course, at that point, nothing had gone wrong, Vivi conceded wryly and it was very likely that Raffaele had viewed her friendship with his sister as harmless. Even so, it had been a mortifyingly happy time for her, she recalled with self-loathing.

Entranced by Raffaele, she had been convinced he was equally interested when he began dropping in on her outings with his sister. Their entire relationship, if it could even be called that, had taken place over only a couple of weeks. She had assumed he was holding back because he didn't want to risk spoiling her friendship with Arianna. She had made so many forgiving assumptions, Vivi recalled, nauseated by the memory of how naive and trusting she had been, believing that he was a generally decent man but, for some reason, exceedingly cautious with women.

And then had come the night of the kiss at Arianna's twentieth birthday party, when he had literally grabbed her out on the terrace where she had been getting some fresh air. He had come out there to lecture her for wandering off alone, as if she were another sister to be schooled and protected like Arianna, and somehow, she didn't quite know how, he had ended up grabbing her instead with a lack of cool and control that had startled her, had startled them *both*, she rather suspected. Yet that single kiss, that he had afterwards apologised for and had treated as trivial, had, ironically, been the most stupendously sexy encounter she had ever shared with a man.

CHAPTER THREE

'WHERE ON EARTH are you going dressed like that?' Zoe exclaimed with a scandalised look as Vivi slid into her concealing trench coat in the small hall of the house they shared. Instantly, Vivi wished she had got into the coat before her sister could even glimpse what she was wearing and her face burned hot with mortification.

'I'm dining with Raffaele. I told you that earlier,' Vivi reminded the younger woman, who bore little resemblance to her, being both small and blonde in colouring.

'Dressed like *that*?' Zoe demanded in disbelief, still staring at the pelmet-length skirt revealing her sibling's very long and shapely legs, the cropped top that showed off the diamond in her navel and the sky-high heels. 'That's the outfit you wore to that insane hen party you went to last winter.'

'*So?*' Vivi flung her hair back in challenge.

'It's very provocative,' Zoe muttered as if Vivi might not have realised that.

'No, it's the perfect outfit to put on for a guy who thinks I'm a tart for hire,' Vivi countered with a defiant lift of her chin.

'Oh, for goodness' sake, Vivi!' Zoe lamented loudly. 'As he's met Grandad, he's got to know how wrong he was by now!'

'No. This is Raffaele di Mancini, who never ever admits to being wrong about anything,' Vivi traded with a lethal gleam of threat and resentment in her bright blue eyes.

'I don't see how dressing like that and giving him entirely the wrong impression is likely to change that,' Zoe admitted ruefully.

'I'm not trying to change *anything*,' Vivi riposted. 'I'm just giving him what he expects and deserves. And I *like* yanking his chain.'

'If you're going to be forced to go through with marrying him, you should be making peace with him,' Zoe opined worriedly. 'I was so hoping that our brother-in-law would find a way out of this mess for us...'

Vivi pursed her lips, thinking of her phone call to her sister, Winnie, before she got dressed. Only her grandfather or their foster parents could pay off the mortgage debt being held over their heads. John and Liz didn't have the money and were too proud and independent to accept the money from anyone else. In popular parlance, it seemed that their goose was cooked as far as wriggling out of the agreement they had made with their grandfather was concerned. He had the sisters tied up tight without wriggle room and with the legal advisers he had on hand that was hardly surprising. Stamboulas Fotakis hadn't become very rich by leaving anything to chance.

'And what are you going to do about Jude?' Zoe continued ruefully.

Vivi compressed her lips with sudden gravity. 'End it. It wasn't going any place anyway. I like him and I think he feels much the same as me.' She shrugged. 'There's just something missing.'

A limo picked her up to ferry her out to dinner and she sat in that opulent leather-upholstered interior checking out the bar appointments and the television before topping up her lipstick. While enjoying that luxury, she was filled with gleeful anticipation at the prospect of Raffaele's likely reaction to being cursed to dine in public with a woman dressed as she was. Raffaele was very old-school and she was convinced they would be meeting at some very exclusive but stodgy and traditional location.

But in that assumption she was swiftly proved wrong for the limo drew up outside a familiar building: the town house that was Raffaele's very imposing London home, which was about twenty times larger than the house she and her sister occupied. Raffaele's, of course, sat off a dignified residential square with a private park in the centre. To Vivi's annoyance, nervous perspiration dampened her body because she hadn't realised she would be anywhere alone with him. Nor was sporting her current outfit in the privacy of his home likely to be the embarrassment for him that she had envisaged.

Raffaele's day had, for some unknown reason, gone excessively slowly for him. Instead of racing past in its usual whirl of urgent appointments, updates and important meetings it had crawled at a snail's pace, irritating him, and he awaited Vivi's arrival with mixed feelings. Tonight, he would get everything sorted out, he reasoned, striving to feel satisfaction over that obvious reality. Tonight, he would do whatever it took to get Vivi to the altar for Arianna's benefit. So, why the hell was he on edge and counting down the hours?

It was not as if Vivi were any great challenge, he told himself grimly. She was a twenty-three-year-old woman with a reasonable education, quick of wit and temper. No big deal, he told himself even as a weird little voice whispered in the back of his brain...*and she wants you.*

Madre di Dio...why the hell had his mind gone in that direction? Lots of women had wanted Raffaele and he accepted that a good ninety per cent of those same women wouldn't have wanted him without the wealth that came with him. That was a fact of life but it was also a fact of life that he had discovered a sexual chemistry with Vivi that had threatened to burn him alive, proving more seductive, more powerful and more dangerous than anything he had ever previously experienced with a woman.

Two years back it had unnerved him just a little to register that a young woman he had believed at the time to be relatively inexperienced could have that effect on him without utilising any obvious wiles. Afterwards, when he had realised how he had been duped, he had been both relieved and enraged and walking away fast hadn't satisfied his need for retaliation. She had played him for a fool with those shy little upward glances, that breathy little giggle that could turn into an oddly entrancing snort, the violet eyes that roamed over him and lingered with what he had interpreted as rather naive sexual curiosity.

But none of that had been *real*, he reminded himself stubbornly. It had all been an act of innocence designed to draw him in, and he would've fallen for that act if she hadn't then been exposed for the greedy little schemer she undoubtedly was. Or *had been*, he adjusted, allowing that the belated discovery that her grandfather was one of the richest men in the world had to have altered her outlook. One thing was certain, Vivi no longer needed to target rich men to improve her lot in life.

He should've known better even when he first met Vivi and believed her to be the ordinary girl she pretended to be, he reflected broodingly. His own family history should, after all, have taught him a harsh enough lesson. His parents had been very happily married, giving him an idyllic childhood in his early years. And then his mother had died suddenly from an aneurysm and his father had been distraught and painfully lonely.

That was when Arianna's mother, Sofia, had sneaked past his once shrewd father's defences. Matteo di Mancini hadn't recognised her for the mercenary degenerate woman she was. All the peace had been sucked out of Raffaele's childhood home with Sofia's tempestuous arrival. His father had married her in a hurry without getting to know her properly and, instead of acknowledging his mistake and divorcing her, he had tried to make the best of a bad bargain. The stress of that deeply unhappy second marriage had most probably led to the older man's premature death from a heart attack.

Grim in the wake of those timely reflections, Raffaele was poised by the fireplace in the formal drawing room when he heard the sounds of Vivi's arrival…the click of high heels on the limestone floor and the quiet murmur of his elderly butler, Willard, as he took her coat. The door opened and Vivi paused in the doorway and that first glimpse literally took his breath away.

Two years back she had never worn revealing clothes around him and now, all of a sudden and when he least expected such a display from her, she was virtually half naked. Working out the reasons behind that sudden change in approach was beyond Raffaele's very masculine reaction to the sight of her at that moment. He was mesmerised. Long, long perfect legs showed to advantage in a very short skirt. A diamond twinkled exotically in her pierced navel, the smooth white skin of her midriff and tiny waist exposed while her small but pert breasts, round as ripe apples, pushed against the figure-hugging fabric of her top. Instantly, Raffaele went as hard as a rock but that, at least, kicked his brain back into gear.

'Good evening,' Vivi breathed a tad shakily, because Raffaele staring at her as he was had always disconcerted her. 'I thought I'd give you a treat.'

But then there had never been a man who disturbed her as much as Raffaele did without even trying. He could lift a well-bred brow or angle up his chin or even widen his eyes slightly as he looked at her and immediately plunge her into discomfiture and the fear that she had done something wrong. She could feel her face colouring up in a horrible blush, because all of a sudden she was feeling horribly self-conscious and underdressed. What had seemed funny and apt back in her bedroom now felt more like self-inflicted humiliation.

'A treat?' Raffaele repeated, brilliant dark eyes still locked to her, roving over the magnificent fall of her copper curls, the even more striking contrast of her hair against her translucent skin and the bright blue eyes below her winged auburn brows.

'Yes. I thought you deserved to get the woman you believe me to be,' she confided. 'Only I expected us to be dining out somewhere and I hoped to embarrass you with this get-up.'

'I'm not embarrassed,' Raffaele murmured, dry-mouthed. On fire with lust, intrigued by her nerve but decidedly *not* embarrassed.

Vivi shrugged a slim shoulder. 'Why would you be in your own home?' she countered ruefully, her disappointment at that truth so obvious to him that he almost laughed.

'It's a shame I don't have a stripper pole,' Raffaele breathed tautly, struggling to keep his wholly inappropriate amusement concealed.

Vivi tossed her head, a string of coiling curls cascading against her cheeks before rearranging themselves across her slight shoulders. He remembered running his fingers through that hair when it was smooth and straight without a hint of curl and the pulse tingling at his groin went even crazier.

'I wouldn't know what to do with a stripper pole,' Vivi admitted regretfully.

'We'll have champagne…' Raffaele informed his butler.

'Champagne? Are we celebrating something?' Vivi queried.

Raffaele rested eyes that were the colour of burnt toffee on her piquant face. 'Our upcoming wedding?' he challenged.

Vivi flung herself down in the corner of a sofa, trying to make herself at home and force herself to relax a little. 'No can do. I can't agree to it. I hate you. I can't possibly do you a favour. It would kill me,' she told him truthfully as a foaming goblet of champagne was presented to her on an actual silver salver. The whole formal process struck her as surreal because it had not occurred to her that in this day and age anyone outside the royal family lived with such traditional regality.

'I will change your mind on that score,' Raffaele assured her confidently.

'One would have to wonder just how you're planning to do that,' Vivi remarked, sipping her champagne, bubbles bursting against her upper lip. 'I am not a woman who is easily swayed.'

Although, admittedly if she *had* been the easily swayed type, Raffaele posed mere feet away in a very sharp designer suit, Vivi ruminated, could probably have achieved the feat. It wasn't fair that he was still downright eye-catching, that his looks hadn't begun to degrade a little with the hint of a paunch or a receding hairline. No, there he was in all his magnificence, drop-dead, gloriously beautiful and lethal as a toxin to her peace of mind. She crossed her legs in haste, innately aware of the hum starting up between them, a fiercely disconcerting reminder of what proximity to Raffaele did to her. She gulped down her champagne in the hope of cooling the heat flooding her and almost winced as she recognised the tingling of her tightening nipples.

That was what Raffaele did to her and mercifully he was the only man who affected her that way, because she loathed the feeling that she was out of control of her own body. It was unnerving and rather humiliating to be physically crushing on him like a schoolgirl. She smiled stiffly as he refilled her glass, determined not to show her inner turmoil.

'You have a beautiful body,' Raffaele said almost prosaically as he straightened again.

'What on earth are you saying that to me for?' Vivi demanded defensively.

'Presumably you wanted me to notice your body or you wouldn't be showing off so much of it,' Raffaele countered drily.

'That wasn't meant to be personal!' Vivi almost spat back at him in rebuke. 'I planned to embarrass you, not show off anything to you!'

'Relax… I'm enjoying the view,' Raffaele murmured silkily. 'It's time for us to move into the dining room and eat.'

Vivi plunged upright with relief and almost toppled back down again as she rocked inelegantly in the very high Perspex wedges she sported.

To her annoyance, Raffaele stretched out a hand to clasp her elbow and steady her. She felt the heat and strength of those long brown fingers right down to the marrow in her bones, she thought fancifully, while an alarming arrow of awareness sliced through her body and coiled into a ball of heat in her pelvis. She glanced up at him on the way out into the hall and encountered stunning dark eyes that glittered as though shot through with diamonds. He had the most amazingly long, thick lashes, she noted abstractedly, her chest tightening as her breathing shorted out. For a split second, meeting those eyes, she wasn't even aware of where she was. A terrifying kind of blankness invaded her brain and she drank deep of her champagne again, desperate to do something with her restless hands.

The dining room, as stately as the drawing room, was splendid enough to command her attention. The room exuded discreet Georgian elegance from the marble fireplace to the opulent drapes at the windows and the beautifully set table, gleaming with crystal and silver and ornamented with fresh flowers.

'This is very formal just for the two of us,' she muttered, even more ill at ease in her clothing against such a backdrop.

'I didn't want to disappoint Willard.'

'Willard?'

'My butler here, inherited from my father and nothing will persuade him to retire,' Raffaele murmured in a rueful undertone. 'He has no family of his own. Over the years, my sister and I have become his family.'

'It's rather sweet that you haven't forced him into retirement,' Vivi commented helplessly, betraying her surprise as she looked across the table at him.

'He was very good to me when I was a child,' Raffaele admitted grudgingly. 'But he does enjoy the ceremony of doing things the same way he did them for my father. He doesn't realise that the world has moved on.'

As Vivi savoured a mouthful of food, she tilted her head back. 'So, you can be kind. What a shame you weren't kind to me!'

Raffaele set his teeth together hard. 'But I am not guilty of having labelled you a prostitute in the press. That was a tabloid invention for a headline, nothing whatsoever to do with me.'

Vivi shrugged. 'But you still believed that of me,' she condemned. 'Even though you had got to know me as Arianna's friend.'

'I *thought* I had got to know you,' Raffaele conceded in scathing interruption.

'You *had* got to know me,' Vivi said again steadily as the second course slid before her. 'You just wanted a scapegoat.'

'I'm not like that,' Raffaele said icily.

Vivi rolled her eyes in expressive disagreement and tucked into her food with surprising appetite. When she had agreed to dine with him, she had had a plan in place. For the sake of her self-esteem, she had to clear her own name with him and force him to see that he had got everything wrong. 'You are exactly like that,' she disagreed. 'You make up your mind about something or someone and you don't revisit the decision.'

'I have a logical mind,' Raffaele countered coolly, noting the way her eyes darkened, her colour lifted and her breathing quickened when she began to get angry.

Vivi sucked in a deep breath and riveted his attention to the natural shift of her small unbound breasts beneath her stretchy top. 'I had only been in that receptionist job for two weeks. It was my very first paid employment and I only took it because I couldn't get anything better in the short term and I needed to work to pay my rent,' Vivi told him resolutely.

A sardonic quirk curling his wide sensual mouth, Raffaele struggled to regain his concentration with the taut peaks of her breasts creating indents in the fabric of her top. He wondered if that was the true intention behind her revealing clothing. An aid to distract him rather than an intended embarrassment? It was very basic, he reasoned with clenched teeth, striving not to linger on the view across the table. He was a red-blooded man and she turned him on hard and fast.

'You don't look like you're listening,' Vivi complained.

'I'm listening,' Raffaele growled.

'Well, you don't have to be so bad-tempered about it!' Vivi tossed at him, pushing away her empty plate and studying him expectantly, her attention welded to his lean, darkly handsome features. 'I'm trying to explain.'

'I didn't ask you to explain anything,' Raffaele incised. 'In fact, I think it would be much more sensible if we *avoid* discussing the past.'

Vivi groaned at that discouraging response and rolled her eyes heavenward again.

'Try not to roll your eyes…it irritates me,' Raffaele warned her.

Vivi clenched her teeth together hard and thrust back her chair to stand up, lifting her champagne glass and saluting him with an ironic look. 'What a charmer you can be,' she replied thinly. 'As I was saying…'

'Very, very *slowly*,' Raffaele slotted in drily.

'Because you weren't listening!' Vivi fired back at him in sharp rebuke. 'And there's no point me talking if you're not listening!'

Raffaele stood up and watched her walk aimlessly across the room, the short skirt swishing above her long slender thighs and accentuating her curvy little behind, the ridiculous shoes merely making the perfection of her legs and delicate ankles more obvious. He released his breath in a controlled hiss, tense and angry about the level of his arousal and on another level outraged by the way she kept up the backchat.

'Get to the point,' he urged impatiently.

Vivi shot him a furious glance over one slim shoulder. 'And I *thought* you had such great manners.'

'Depends on the company I'm keeping.' Raffaele compressed his sculpted lips, sentencing himself to silence once he appreciated that fighting with Vivi was only going to make his goal of marrying her more difficult to achieve.

Vivi spun, blue eyes violet with rage. 'And we all know, of course, what kind of company you think I am.'

'You were telling me about your employment in the brothel.'

'The brothel was at the back in an attached building that I never had access to. It had a separate entrance. How was I supposed to know it was there?' Vivi demanded, emptying her glass and setting it down with a sharp little snap at the end of the polished table. 'I worked in the modelling agency, which was a legitimate modelling agency.'

'*Legitimate?* A place with a photographer who persuaded Arianna to take her clothes off for the camera for glamour photos?' Raffaele scoffed with disdain. 'Do I really look that stupid?'

'You may not look it but you are!' Vivi flashed back without hesitation. 'Arianna made an unwise decision but that was her call, not mine. She didn't discuss stripping for the camera with me at any time. All I did was make the stupid appointment for her.'

'And did you get commission for luring her into the studio?' Raffaele derided.

'Good grief, Raffaele... I was a receptionist, not a pimp!' Vivi gasped. 'I didn't lure her anywhere. Why would I have?'

'Because those naked photos were a means of profit in unscrupulous hands,' Raffaele told her grimly. 'I had to buy them back at a hugely inflated price to protect Arianna because the contract she unwisely signed had small print she didn't bother to read.'

Vivi nodded reluctantly, frustrated that she seemed to be getting nowhere with him when it came to the matter of her own lack of involvement in his sister's misfortunes at the agency. 'Well, I'm sorry about that but it's still got nothing to do with me. I was just one of the administrative staff.'

'Why can't you just come clean?' Raffaele raked at her in a raw undertone. 'I'm not going to tell tales to your grandfather. You were not a receptionist, you were one of the models doing escort work on the side.'

'A model?' Vivi exclaimed in angry disbelief, her hands coiling into furious fists. 'I've never modelled in my life!'

'Well, then, if you're sticking to that story,' Raffaele murmured in a silky purr that ran down her spine like a spectral caress, 'perhaps you'd care to explain how the press managed to capture you on camera wearing a designer outfit that *they* priced as having cost thousands of pounds? How did a humble receptionist afford clothes that expensive?'

Vivi frowned and rolled her eyes at him again. 'She didn't. Everything I wore once belonged to your sister. She cleared out her wardrobe and insisted on giving me her cast-offs. As we're almost the exact same size, it was wonderful for me because, fresh from university, I didn't own many clothes and Arianna was sick of seeing me in the same dress when we went out.'

Raffaele had lost colour. 'I don't believe you.'

'Phone her and ask if you must have verification,' Vivi urged angrily. 'My goodness, Raffaele, can't you accept and believe anything I tell you?'

'You were wearing second-hand clothing?' Raffaele pressed incredulously.

'I buy second-hand stuff in charity shops all the time…or I used to,' Vivi muttered in the spirit of honesty integral to her outspoken nature. 'Are you always so prejudiced against people who have less money than you? Do you always think the worst of them?'

'I am not prejudiced,' Raffaele bit out grittily.

'Oh, yes, you are!' Vivi hurled back, stalking up to him to poke a forefinger right into his shirt front. 'If I cut you in half, I'd find prejudice running right through you in a seam of gold. According to your view of the world, only rich people have principles and self-respect. You thought the worst of me without good reason.'

'I had good reason,' Raffaele framed wrathfully. 'And don't touch me again.'

'It was just a tiny little poke!' Vivi's forefinger stabbed his chest again because she couldn't resist the temptation. 'Stop being so blasted stuffy!'

Raffaele's eyes flashed like a storm warning laced with lightning and he grabbed her up against him. 'I'll show you stuffy.'

'Fighting words!' Vivi scorned.

And then his mouth crashed down on hers and the world went dark and she teetered in her high heels, legs suddenly as boneless as grass stalks. His tongue pierced the moist interior of her mouth and set off a cascade of sensations that made her every skin cell tingle with excitement. Her eyes slid closed, her whole body gripped by an elemental force of pleasurable anticipation. She tried to fight it off, for an instant she even tried to pull back but her limbs were boneless, her body overheated and desperate to be crushed to the hard, unyielding strength of his.

'What are we doing?' she muttered shakily, briefly coming up for air.

'What we should have done the minute you arrived,' Raffaele growled, knowing he was dangerously out of control but unexpectedly enjoying that sensation of risk.

'What cave did you come out of this morning?' Vivi

sniped while locked to him like a second skin, innately aware of every muscular and powerful line of his big body.

Raffaele stared down at the sultry reddened line of her full mouth and the warning voices in the back of his head receded into silence. He wanted her. He wanted her as he had never wanted any woman before and he wasn't in the mood to deny himself. And colliding with those violet eyes clouded with passion as he went in to taste her mouth again, he knew that she wanted him just as much.

Good grief, he could kiss, Vivi conceded in a daze. Her head swam while her body craved the simple plea-sure of being touched. Not something she had ever al-lowed herself to feel before but then she hadn't been tempted before. Now wildly conscious of the heat gath-ering at the heart of her and the tightness of her nipples, she was trembling, stunned by the effect he had on her. An explosion of heat mushroomed up inside her as he worked her mouth, penetrating, withdrawing, setting up a chain reaction through her quivering length.

A lean hand probed beneath her skirt and she stopped breathing as he touched her. Without her volition her thighs locked round his hand and she gasped, stroked in that one place that drove her absolutely crazy, her lips parting beneath his as his fingers tugged away the crotch of her knickers and located the dampness she couldn't control. Her body jackknifed in his hold and she jerked, gasping in response.

'You're incredibly sexy,' Raffaele husked.

And Vivi gazed up at him, helplessly impressed by

any form of compliment from Raffaele. The space between her legs was pounding out a drumbeat of craving stronger than anything she had ever felt and she couldn't think straight, she couldn't think beyond that terrible unrelenting hunger assailing her. 'So are you,' she muttered dazedly.

'I have never wanted any woman the way I want you,' he admitted in a driven undertone.

Vivi's eyes gleamed with satisfaction because there was a wonderful symmetry about that admission. He wanted her as much as she wanted him. He didn't like feeling that way any more than she did and that made them fully *equal* for the very first time...

CHAPTER FOUR

RAFFAELE LIFTED HER up off her feet into his arms and a stifled sound of surprise escaped her. But his sheer physical strength, not to mention his assurance, exhilarated her and sent her mind roaming in all sorts of intimate directions.

'A caveman lurks inside that fancy business suit of yours,' Vivi whispered, gazing up at him with instinctive appreciation as he settled her down on the ornamental sofa below one of the windows.

A caveman who only emerged around her, Raffaele adjusted, refusing to think. Even so, he didn't do casual sex. Nor did he succumb to sudden impulses or give way to temptation. But, nevertheless, here he was with Vivi in his arms and a fire alarm wouldn't have persuaded him to put her down again anywhere but on a horizontal surface. Some stuff didn't need to be agonised over, some things between men and women weren't complicated, he reasoned fiercely. Sex was just sex and their physical connection was remarkable and could well lead to them reaching agreement on the wedding her grandfather was demanding. Do you really *believe* that? a voice asked in his hind brain. And he knew he didn't, but he didn't much care either. Aroused to the point of pain, he was way beyond utilising logic.

For a split second, when he came down beside her, Vivi froze because her natural defences were suddenly all loudly screeching, 'What are you doing?'

Raffaele, however, was more perceptive than she would've given him credit for because instead of grabbing her again he tilted her face up, scanning her anxious eyes. 'Cold feet?' he prompted, tensing at that prospect.

'I don't get cold feet,' Vivi proclaimed with pride, feeling foolish about her momentary indecision. Insane curiosity was pulling at her because she badly wanted to know what intimacy would be like with him. If he was using her, she would also be using him and it was a plus that she would never have to see him again.

'*Madre di Dio...* I hope not,' Raffaele countered with heartfelt honesty, bending down to taste her mouth again with hungry, driving urgency.

Straight away the conflagration of heat came back and blew her away. Thought hung suspended while an expert hand disposed of the barriers between them. In fact, Vivi didn't notice because Vivi was in a world of her own, a world of fiercely seductive physical need and sensation. He pushed her top out of his path and palmed her breasts, addressing his mouth to her straining pink nipples, and her temperature rose to an insane height, her body writhing of its own volition while he teased the tender flesh between her thighs with a skill that she was defenceless against. She gasped, moaned, clawed him down to her with an impatient hand, pale slender fingers locking into the crisp luxuriance of his short black hair.

Excitement gripped her in a heady wave as her hips rose in an arc of colossal craving, as if there were some distant point she would die if she didn't reach. He crushed her parted lips, delved deep with his tongue, a shudder of violent arousal raking through his lean, powerful frame while she yanked at his tie, almost strangling him before he ripped it off for her. She needed to touch his skin, she needed to touch him so badly that not being able to actually hurt. While he kissed her, she struggled with his shirt until he tore it free, sending several buttons bouncing, unnoticed by either of them.

'You're burning me up,' he groaned.

Vivi spread her hands wide on his lean bronzed chest, overpowered by the heat of his skin and his sheer muscular development as he leant over her obligingly. 'You *are* hot,' she whispered tongue-in-cheek.

And he got it, a sudden slashing grin banishing the often forbidding aspect of his lean, strong face, the febrile line of colour over his exotic cheekbones darkening. His thumb stroked across the most sensitive spot on her whole body and she jerked, suddenly mindless again, and his mouth engulfed hers. She wanted more, more, simply *more*. Nothing more elaborate distinguished her febrile thoughts. His sheer passion had shocked her and then delighted her but the excitement he evoked overwhelmed her.

Raffaele didn't have a condom. She would be on

the pill, he told himself, reluctant to take a break for a trip upstairs in case the impulsive beauty in his arms changed her mind—and it would kill him if she changed her mind! Of course, she would be on the pill or the implant or one of the other contraceptive options available to women, he assumed, tilting her slender thighs back with impatient hands and plunging into her with all the strength and energy of a man turned on to the point of madness.

A startling yelp escaped Vivi as a jolt of pain greeted that intimate invasion and she squeezed her eyes tightly closed, mortified by her outburst.

Raffaele had frozen in the act of penetration. 'Did I hurt you?'

'No, of course you didn't,' she declared, wanting to conceal her lack of experience, which struck her as deeply uncool at her age.

'Then…er…why—?' he began.

'Got carried away by enthusiasm,' Vivi lied but she could feel her face burning like hellfire at the fib. 'That hurt,' she mouthed in total silence as she buried her face in his neck, drinking in the achingly sexy scent of him with all the enthusiasm she had claimed because he smelled so incredibly good, all hot and musky with an undertone of designer cologne that was yummy.

'*Grazie a Dio*… Thank God,' Raffaele groaned in relief, shifting his lean hips in a motion that stirred up nerve cells that had run screaming from his initial thrust, sending instead an intriguing cascade of simmering sensation travelling through her lower body.

Her tension evaporated, liquid heat sizzling through

her veins, lighting her up from inside out. He slid deeper into her and began to move and the hot, sweet pleasure began to gather in her pelvis, building and building like a fire being teased into flames. A kind of wonder gripped her as the frantic throes of arousal rose again and he released a guttural groan of satisfaction, muttering something indistinct in Italian, leaning down to crush her mouth under his again. For an instant she had thought in disappointment that he was done, that that was that, that all the fuss she had heard about was just stories to temp the inexperienced and then his pace picked up and the whole mood changed.

Raffaele rose over her, tipping her thighs back over his shoulders to pound into her in a raw demonstration of uncontrolled hunger. Her head fell back, the heat in her lower body spreading and mushrooming up inside her fast in a shocking surge that couldn't be contained. Her heart started to race, breathlessness tightening her throat as the excitement climbed and her body clenched around him with an unbearable tightness. His urgency infiltrated every inch of her, dominating and controlling her in a way she had never dreamt, and then the heat exploded inside her and sent her flying. Contractions of pleasure convulsed her in an intoxicating wave that made her cry out in surprise and fall back, sated, in delirious delight, to revel in the aftershocks.

'That was incredible,' Raffaele said for her, brushing her tumbled copper curls back from her damp brow, his dark deep voice raw and breathless as he lifted back from her to release her from his crushing weight.

An odd little silence fell and Vivi lifted eyelids that

felt heavy because she was in a drowsy daze after that insane surge of sensual pleasure. Raffaele was frowning down at her. 'There's blood on you…'

A deep flush of mortification swept up over Vivi's expressive face, her consternation unhidden. She sat up in haste to hug her knees, her mane of curls tumbling round her like a cloak. 'Is there?' she tried to say coolly but her voice emerged as hesitant and awkward as she felt. 'I was a virgin. I wasn't expecting actual bl—'

'A…*virgin*?' Raffaele exclaimed incredulously, ready to argue with her statement and then freezing to logically consider the facts, not to mention her grandfather's warning. A warning to which he had not paid the slightest heed, he acknowledged sickly, because he had discounted the older man's view of his grandchild where it conflicted with his own convictions. To have his convictions suddenly proved utterly wrong when he least expected it wasn't an experience that Raffaele had had very often in life and it absolutely knocked him sideways.

'Yes, no big deal,' Vivi dismissed hurriedly, scrambling off the sofa to gather up her clothing and pull it on at speed, while simultaneously attempting to shrug a careless shoulder.

'It was a very big deal if you were still a virgin at your age,' Raffaele contradicted without hesitation.

'I was just never that into…er…sex,' Vivi muttered in a quelling tone. 'And don't ask me why I'm different with you because I don't know the answer to that.'

'It's called chemistry,' Raffaele breathed, still struggling to get a handle on the sheer shock value of Vivi, with her diamond-studded navel and Perspex heels, being a complete innocent. 'It affected *my* judgement as well.'

Vivi shrugged again. 'What's done is done.'

She sounded very young and very sure of that and Raffaele suppressed a groan, suddenly feeling very much older than his thirty years as he zipped his trousers. 'It may not be because in the grip of that chemistry I made a rash decision. Assuming that you would be on birth control and because I had nothing conveniently available, I omitted to use contraception.'

'But I'm not on birth control.' She gasped and one hand flew up to her mouth to cover it in a show of anxiety. 'And that means—'

'That whatever happens, I'm with you every step of the way. When I make a mistake I own up and do what I can to rectify it,' Raffaele delivered grimly as he pulled on his shirt.

Vivi wasn't enamoured of being labelled a mistake. 'There's nothing you can do to rectify this mistake.'

Raffaele's wide sensual mouth quirked. 'There's no point agonising right now over something we can't change either. Thankfully we're not frightened teenagers.'

'Yes…er…that's true,' Vivi conceded grudgingly. 'But I just can't believe you took that risk with me.'

'In the aftermath…' Raffaele rested brilliant dark eyes on her flushed little face, against which her bright blue eyes were even more striking than usual '…neither can I. I chose to assume that it wouldn't be a risk, which was irrational.'

'Didn't think you *did* irrational stuff,' Vivi broke in helplessly.

'Don't mock,' Raffaele urged. 'It's as much of a surprise to me as it is to you. Why are you putting your shoes on?'

Vivi lifted her head, eyes widening. 'To go home?'

Raffaele frowned. 'You're not going home—you're staying the night.'

Her blue eyes opened very wide as she gazed rather blankly back at him from the sofa where she sat. 'Zoe will be expecting me home.'

'So, phone her,' Raffaele advised, pushing his advantage where he saw it because their encounter had off-balanced her and he didn't want her taking refuge again behind her usually aggressive façade.

Put on the spot, Vivi hesitated and then she dug out her phone. Their intimacy on the sofa had seemed a touch too casual and juvenile to her taste while staying the night struck her as more adult and acceptable. She had slept with Raffaele di Mancini and shock waves were still racing through her at that awareness. She didn't know how it had happened and that unnerved her but she didn't want to decide it was a mistake either. Much better to accept it as just another one of life's experiences, she told herself firmly. Why should she make a fuss or feel guilty about something as normal and everyday as sex?

'I won't be home until tomorrow,' she told her sister. 'I've had too much champagne…far too much champagne,' she repeated, thinking about that with a brow that pleated because as a rule she didn't drink.

'You were drinking champagne with Mancini?' Zoe exclaimed in disbelief.

'It was lovely champagne,' Vivi said ruefully before she rang off and glanced across at Raffaele, whose shirt was still hanging open on his broad bronzed chest, revealing the slabs of lean muscle roping his abdomen. 'I don't usually drink much. I think I was drunk.'

'No, you weren't!' Raffaele contradicted with vigour. 'I don't have sex with drunken women. Stop looking for excuses. Just accept it for what it was.'

But she didn't *know* what it was, which was the real problem. It was not as though she had stayed a virgin for a specific reason. When she had been younger and less cynical she had, admittedly, dreamt of falling in love before she had sex for the first time, but even then she had been in no hurry after a foster parent had once tried to touch her inappropriately, an experience that had laid a seedy veil over any sexual thoughts for Vivi. Furthermore, she hadn't fallen in love, and even though love had happened for her older sister, Winnie had had to walk a long stony road to finally find her happy ending.

Vivi had stopped dreaming of love once she'd registered that loving a man often came with pain and disappointment. Indeed, loving meant being vulnerable and, if Vivi could help it, she never ever allowed herself to be as vulnerable as she had been as a child. Back then she had often been at the mercy of adults who insisted that they knew what was best for her even though they so obviously didn't, because she would always end up

in yet another unhappy living situation. Trusting anyone beyond her sisters was a challenge for her.

'What was it, then?' Vivi persisted.

'*Non importa*...no matter,' Raffaele overruled with
determination as he bent and simply scooped her up off
the sofa to carry her to the door, having decided that
that particular conversation was only likely to lead them
into even murkier waters.

'What on earth are you doing?' Vivi demanded.

'Taking you upstairs to a shower and a proper bed,'
Raffaele confided.

That programme sounded remarkably attractive to
Vivi at that moment. She let him carry her upstairs,
marvelling at the new intimacy between them. Of
course that was the sex, she assumed. Some comfort
that would be if she conceived a child, she reasoned
worriedly. Winnie had had an unplanned pregnancy.
As a result, Vivi was all too aware of the discomforts
of pregnancy and the burden of a baby's constant demands and she most definitely didn't want to follow in
her sister's footsteps.

But in assuming that sex had made Raffaele more
demonstrative, Vivi could not have been more wrong.
Vivi had just proven every one of Raffaele's convictions
about her to be mistaken and he was reeling from the
discovery that he was not as infallible a judge of character as he had believed himself to be.

It had finally dawned on him that Vivi *could* simply
have been a receptionist at that agency and the ordinary, if beautiful, young woman she had purported to
be, polished up to a deceptively exclusive level by his

sister's cast-off clothing. And if that was true, it meant he had misjudged her on every front. That was a bitter pill for him to swallow.

'I still hate you, you know,' Vivi warned him almost chattily as he set her down, barefoot, in a fabulous contemporary bathroom.

'I can live with that,' Raffaele assured her, unwilling to argue with the obvious reality that naturally she hated him when he had wronged her. He might not have called her a prostitute but he had not spoken up in her defence at the time either because he had blamed her for his sister's mistakes and had been determined to ensure that Arianna wasn't dragged into the same scandal.

Closing the door, he left her alone and Vivi breathed again. She was already struggling to accept what had happened between them. She had slept with Raffaele di Mancini, a man she hated like poison. How did that make sense? But then there had been no sense whatsoever in the encounter. She had been foolish, *he* had been foolish and he had surprised her by admitting the fact. She stripped and stepped into the shower but the minute the water came on and hit her from all directions in one of those technically advanced showers, destined to be a cleansing spa experience rather than a simple washing facility, she stepped out of it again in haste because she didn't want to get her hair wet and couldn't be bothered fiddling to work out the controls.

She ran a bath instead, stepped in and folded down with a slight wince as the tenderness between her legs made its presence felt. Yes, she had had sex for the first time and, with hindsight, it would've made more sense to warn him to ensure he tempered his passion. Vivi pressed cool hands to her hot cheeks and marvelled that she had given way to temptation. But he was right when he said they had strong chemistry. The kind of hunger he awakened in Vivi was so primal and so powerful she hadn't been able to withstand it. Once he touched her she had been lost, her entire being surrendered instead to the need he had ignited in her. She washed, dried herself and peered out into the empty bedroom, which was lit by lamps on either side of the bed.

In spite of the fact that she had a boyfriend, she had slept with another man, she ruminated guiltily. It didn't matter that the chemistry between her and Jude was as tepid as cold tea. What mattered was loyalty and she, a woman who valued loyalty, had been disloyal. She would end their relationship the following evening. In the circumstances, honesty was the best policy.

Exhaustion was beginning to creep over her, exacerbated, she suspected, by the champagne she had imbibed and the mad rush of conflicting thoughts and reactions assailing her. She would go to bed, sleep, she told herself heavily, there was nothing more to be said or done or decided right at that very moment.

Raffaele took in the vision of Vivi lying in his bed, her mane of hair fanned out across the white pillows, her luscious mouth pink and ripe from his kisses, her delicate features smooth in relaxation and involuntarily, he was spellbound. *Maledizione*…she was beautiful. Why was he allowing that truth to mess with his brain? At the start of the evening he had had a clear objective, which was to persuade Vivi, by any means within his power, to marry him. What had happened to that goal? Why had he even brought her to his bedroom instead of to one of the guest rooms? When too had he ever lost control like that with a woman? When had he ever run such a risk?

Self-loathing and a rare sense of failure attacked Raffaele in the aftermath of those unfamiliar thoughts. He had had sex instead of concentrating on protecting his sister. Even worse, his already thorny dealings with Vivi would only become more fraught and complex because they had become intimate.

His phone rang at dawn when he was already lying awake in a guest bed, watching the light rise beyond the windows to pierce the edges of the blinds. Reasoning that it had to be some kind of emergency because very few people had access to his private number, he answered it immediately. 'Mancini.'

'It's Stam Fotakis,' the older man grated. 'I'm calling you to inform you that the wedding will take place in three weeks, on the twenty-fifth.'

Raffaele was frowning. 'But—' he began.

'No buts, no *arguments*!' Stam ranted angrily down the phone. 'My granddaughter spent the night with you and the date of the wedding is now fixed. I warned you. That dossier on your sister goes to the press this weekend unless you can confirm that date!'

Within minutes, in the bedroom next door, Vivi was enjoying a similar rude awakening. 'Grandad?' she said sleepily, barely half awake. 'It's very early to be phoning.'

'You spent the night with Mancini. You're getting married to him on the twenty-fifth of this month and there won't be any more arguments on that score! Is that understood?'

Her face scarlet, Vivi was now sitting bolt upright in the bed. 'How do you know where I spent the night?' she gasped.

'Your security team,' Stam delivered curtly. 'There will be no further discussion about this matter.'

Vivi had never got dressed in such haste and never before with such distaste for the garments she was forced to put back on. The outfit, which had seemed such a good idea the night before, now filled her with embarrassment. Had Raffaele read the short skirt and the rest of it as some sort of a come-on? It didn't really matter now though, did it? *She* had lost control, *she* had failed to call a halt, *she* had defied her own intelligence to continue that monumental mistake. She couldn't blame alcohol, she couldn't blame Raffaele, who was probably as programmed to take advantage of a willing woman as any other man; no, she could only blame herself. It seemed a fitting punishment that she now had to slip out of the house and take the walk of shame in those hateful Perspex heels! But the worst punishment of all for Vivi was the utterly mortifying knowledge that her grandfather was also aware that she had spent the night with Raffaele.

Vivi was halfway down the stairs, picking her way as quietly as she could, when Raffaele emerged without warning from a doorway. Her expressive face flamed, her eyes cloaking, soft mouth compressing into a tense line. Even in that single flaring glance she noticed that he looked amazing, all sleek and dark and spectacular in a dark grey suit, cut to enhance his lean, powerful build and accentuate his superb carriage. He emanated rock-solid assurance and it set her teeth on edge because she was feeling ratty and hunted and insecure.

'Did you get a wake-up call too?' Raffaele enquired softly.

'I'm in a bit of a hurry, actually, so I won't keep you.'

'It's a Saturday morning, so I can't imagine why you should be in a rush. Join me for breakfast,' he told her, striding back into the dining room.

Vivi paused in the doorway. 'Er...thanks, but that doesn't suit. If I could just get my coat...'

'I'll drop you home after breakfast.'

And there it was again, that habit of Raffaele's that made Vivi want to tear her hair out and scream. He didn't listen to what he didn't want to hear, he just moved on past it to repeat his own wishes.

'I said no, thanks,' Vivi reminded him thinly.

In emphasis, Raffaele yanked out a dining chair for her and studied her expectantly. 'Be reasonable, *cara*.'

And without warning, Vivi was made to feel like a child caught in the act of trying to run away to escape a punishment, and that analogy was too humiliating to be endured. Tensing even more, she moved forward on wooden legs and settled stiffly into the seat. 'I have nothing more to say to you.'

'*Non importa*.... I have plenty to say to you,' Raffaele countered, smooth as silk, as his butler appeared at her elbow to offer her a choice of tea, coffee or hot chocolate.

In need of something sweet to bolster her, Vivi chose hot chocolate and reached for toast.

'According to your grandfather, our wedding will be taking place on the twenty-fifth,' Raffaele informed her.

'But I don't listen to his commands when they conflict with what I want,' she parried stubbornly as she buttered her toast, struggling not to think about what her refusal to comply might cost her foster parents.

Winnie had bitten the bullet and married Eros even though it was the last thing she had wanted at the time. Why should she rate her pride higher than Winnie had? Why couldn't she play her part and fall into line for the sake of peace, as Winnie had? Perhaps it was because when she was young she had too often found herself bereft of choice. And now when she was told to do something she didn't agree with she wanted to fight against it every step of the way.

'And if I threaten to make redundancies at Hacketts Tech? And I should be frank, redundancies are required there. The business is overstaffed,' he informed her coolly.

'You're threatening me…'

'I'm threatening you,' Raffaele agreed with a harsh edge to his accented drawl, his brilliant dark eyes veiled by a thick screen of lashes.

Vivi thought frantically about John and Liz and their need for a secure home where they could continue looking after troubled adolescents and helping them into adulthood. Yes, she certainly owed them a debt for the healing regime they had given her because being constantly angry, distrustful and fearful, as she had once been, only made the world an even more scary place. And what about her work colleagues? People had mortgages and rent to pay, loans to keep up, holidays booked, children to raise. The sudden loss of stable employment could devastate lives and that stress could surely destroy relationships as well. Raffaele was putting enormous power into her hands, power she hated him for giving her because to her mind his power to threaten redundancies deprived her of the power to say no to the wedding he and her grandfather were determined to stage.

'So, if I was to say yes…what would happen?' she pressed in a driven surge. 'No redundancies?'

'I could put a stay on them for the immediate future.'

'A *permanent* stay,' Vivi bargained, barely believing that she was finally agreeing to the fake wedding she had long resisted.

'I can't agree to permanent,' Raffaele countered levelly. 'The bottom line must be business and profit.'

'Not for me, it's not. For me, it's people!' Vivi argued with spirit.

'I could put a stay on redundancies for the first year,' Raffaele proffered.

'Three years!' Vivi suggested.

Raffaele frowned. 'Too long. In that time, Hacketts Tech could go under,' he warned her, filling her with consternation for she had not previously appreciated that the firm could already be struggling for survival.

'Eighteen months, then…and the staff get plenty of warning of what's coming,' she bargained in desperation.

Raffaele angled back in his chair, brilliant dark eyes alight as a starry night sky. 'Eighteen months with full disclosure,' he negotiated. 'And on the twenty-fifth we get married.'

'*Fake* married,' Vivi reminded him drily.

'Unless you turn out to be pregnant, in which case all bets will be off,' Raffaele murmured curtly. 'Because that development would be a game-changer.'

'That would be a nightmare,' Vivi contradicted with a tiny lurch of fear because the prospect of pregnancy and motherhood unnerved her. 'But it's not likely to happen, is it?'

Raffaele lifted and dropped a shoulder with the lithe, fluid elegance that was so much a part of him. 'I wouldn't like to call it. It's not a situation I've been in before. How soon will you know?'

Her face warming, Vivi engaged in some fast calculations and unselfconsciously counted on her fingers beneath Raffaele's increasingly incredulous scrutiny, for maths had never been one of Vivi's strengths. 'In about ten days.'

'We'll visit a doctor together. I'll arrange it and that way we'll know exactly where we stand,' Raffaele decreed.

'That's not necessary. There are tests that can be done at home.'

'When it comes to accurate results I prefer to trust

the medical profession,' Raffaele overruled without hesitation.

Vivi breathed in so deep to contain her temper that she marvelled that she didn't take flight like a balloon. She gritted her teeth and focused on her toast, even though it was turning to sawdust inside her dry mouth. How had she contrived to become intimate with a man who enraged her to such a degree? Every time he laid down the letter of the law according to Raffaele she wanted to punch him. Had people always listened respectfully to his commands and done as he told them to do? Had no living person ever contrived to punch a hole in that armour of arrogance he wore? Why did he always believe he was right?

But what did that matter when she had finally been forced to give her consent? Her conscience had made her agree to his terms, she acknowledged unhappily. He had blackmailed her without an ounce of shame or compassion. How could she possibly stand back in silence while people lost their jobs when he was giving her the power to minimise that blow as far as was possible? She wasn't callous enough to shirk the responsibility he had put on her shoulders, she reflected ruefully.

Unfortunately, the repercussions of her decision to capitulate would spread like the ripples that followed a rock being thrown into a pool. Zoe would be caught up in the backwash and put under pressure to become the third and final bride. Her grandfather would be satisfied, although only to *some* extent, she conceded uneasily, recalling his censorious phone call earlier. Heat flushed her troubled face, warm pink chasing the pallor from her taut cheeks. It was a source of serious embarrassment to her to accept that Stamboulas Fotakis was equally aware of her miscalculation.

Miscalculation? Vivi questioned her use of that word on another tide of self-loathing because there had been nothing calculating in anything she had done. Indeed, reason and restraint had been blown out of the water by passion, a passion beyond anything she had ever expected to feel. A passion that in retrospect terrified her. She had tried to excuse herself by blaming it all on the champagne but she hadn't drunk enough of it to use that justification and she knew it.

Raffaele watched Vivi like a hawk, seeing the fleeting expressions chase across her delicate features, curious as to what was skimming through that agile little brain of hers. He was also wondering why he wasn't feeling triumphant that he seemed to have finally contrived to avert the threat aimed at destroying his sister's happiness. Instead he simply felt angry, more coldly angry than he had ever guessed he could feel. He was livid with Stam Fotakis for his crude blackmailing tactics but even more incensed that Vivi had forced him to stoop to the same distasteful level for the first time in his life.

And what if she conceived his child? He released his breath in a slow hiss of determined denial at that possibility. What were the odds? He tried to picture a baby but the only one he could recall was Arianna shrieking through her baptism in the family chapel, a troubled little bundle wrapped in heirloom lace in her unrepentant mother's arms while his father valiantly strove to behave as though it were normal to have a wife beside him strung out on drugs.

Raffaele had been eight years old then and that was the closest he had ever come to a baby. He *should* have been more responsible with Vivi. Lost in the grip of lust, however, he had been intolerably careless. At that point, he censored his brooding reflections and told himself off for assuming the worst. Fate had made him very lucky in business. Why shouldn't he be equally lucky in his private life?

CHAPTER FIVE

'SHE'S *OUT*?' RAFFAELE queried, despising the emphasis he laid on that telling word and the almost frightened look that froze the tiny doll-like blonde in front of him.

'Didn't she mention it?' Zoe Mardas pressed, her discomfiture unhidden.

Raffaele didn't bother to admit that he hadn't spoken to Vivi since the day she'd agreed to marry him. He was fairly sure that she had blocked his number on her phone. She had left him no option other than to arrive on her doorstep. And he had to speak to her before the wedding because it was impossible for him to keep that wedding a secret, which meant that all his relatives would be attending and caught up in the same charade with him.

'Do you know where she is?' Raffaele persisted, recognising that Vivi's kid sister was a soft touch. 'I could speak to her there.'

Zoe flushed and stepped off one foot onto the other like a cat being forced over hot coals. 'I'm afraid that wouldn't be suitable.'

Raffaele frowned, his lean bronzed features darkening. 'Why wouldn't it be suitable?'

'Because she's with her boyfriend,' Zoe whispered shakily, her eyes locking to him with unhidden anxiety as if she expected that admission to turn him into a raging beast.

'Her boyfriend,' Raffaele repeated without any expression at all, trusting neither his voice nor his face in receipt of that news. 'Then I'll wait,' he announced with assurance.

'Oh…er… I don't think she'll be expecting that,' Zoe muttered uneasily.

Which was exactly why Raffaele was determined to do it. He strode into the reception room Zoe indicated and turned round to give the young woman a reassuring smile. 'Just forget I'm here.'

'Would you like coffee…or anything?' his reluctant hostess almost whispered, clearly wishing he would vanish but too scared of her own shadow to argue with him.

'No, thank you. I'll be fine,' Raffaele declared, taking a stance by the window to gaze down into the street below, marvelling that the fiery Vivi could have such a little mouse of a sibling. How much easier would his challenge have been with such a woman?

Oddly enough though, he registered in surprise, he respected Vivi's sheer fearlessness and her need to rise to every fresh challenge. She was no easy touch. Even so, a boyfriend she had not chosen to mention and with only two weeks to go before the wedding, evidently, she was *still* seeing the boyfriend. How was he supposed to feel about that? Just over a week ago she had been a virgin, uninvolved in a sexual relationship with anyone.

But then she had given herself to Raffaele and, as far as he was concerned, that *changed* everything. After that encounter with him, had she then chosen to practise what she had learned and become intimate with her boyfriend as well? Why else had she kept quiet about the man's existence?

But if she had slept with the boyfriend as well, what was it to him? A knot of hard black rage twisted deep inside Raffaele at the very idea of her with another man. Some sort of weird possessiveness had ensnared him once he'd realised he was Vivi's first lover, he decided in exasperation, because for the first time ever he was feeling territorial over a woman. That acknowledgement made his teeth grit because he wasn't and never had been that kind of guy. Sex had always been easy come, easy go with him and he moved on to the next woman without a backward glance. He didn't like ties and he didn't attach ties or expectations to the women who discreetly shared his bed. But he had not and would not have touched another woman since that night with Vivi because he recognised that, however little he liked it, he and Vivi were currently in a relationship and it would be wrong for him to have sex with anyone else. But, evidently, Vivi did not make the same moral distinction.

She had not been honest with him and that infuriated him. She had also closed down all communication with him. Having set about forcing a meeting, he was only now discovering that she was seeing another man and had carefully kept that a secret. Of course, he didn't trust her. How could he? The dark rage in Raffaele climbed closer to the surface.

Vivi received the warning text from Zoe midway through what was proving to be a very trying evening with Jude. Fresh from a week abroad competing in a martial arts tournament and having won a medal, Jude had been in the mood to celebrate over drinks. As soon as she could, Vivi had given him the story she had decided was best in the circumstances, admitting that she had met someone else while he was away. Jude had, seemingly, taken the news well but had blocked her every polite attempt to cut the evening short, pointing out that they could still surely be friends. Guilt had made her acquiesce while the prospect of having to deal with Raffaele once she finally got home made Vivi break out in a cold sweat.

Since that breakfast with him when she'd caved into the inevitability of marrying him, she had steered clear of both Raffaele and her grandfather. At her grandfather's expense she had gone out and purchased a wildly expensive wedding gown complete with all the required accessories. She would play her part in the wedding and that would be that. Tearing herself up about Raffaele or the actual wedding was foolish when she didn't have a choice. Winnie had echoed that view, reasoning that making too much of the necessity was pointless while also commenting at the same time that Raffaele's use of blackmail was complete overkill.

Thinking with bitter contempt of just how far Raffaele was prepared to go to make a killer profit, Vivi stalked into the lounge of her home. Raffaele stood very tall in the window embrasure. He settled shimmering dark golden eyes on her and gooseflesh prickled at the nape of her neck. He had a dark five o'clock shadow that merely enhanced the wide, sensual shape of his beautiful mouth. She remembered the crash and burn effect of that mouth on hers and nervous perspiration dampened the valley between her breasts.

'Where were you?' he demanded succinctly, scanning her lithe, long-legged appearance in jeans, a casual top and knee-high boots.

'That's none of your business,' Vivi declared, tilting her chin. 'I agreed to marry you. I didn't agree to keep you informed of my every move!'

Raffaele flung his wide shoulders back and lifted his arrogant dark head high, ebony brows set level, lean, strong face grim. 'You didn't mention that you had a boyfriend either!'

Zoe must've told him about Jude, Vivi realised in dismay, wishing that her sister had included that revealing information in her text message. But Vivi dismissed her unease and tossed her head, copper curls bouncing across her cheeks and her shoulders. 'Well, what does that have to do with you?' she enquired shortly.

'We're getting married in two weeks.'

'But it'll be a fake, not a real wedding,' Vivi reminded him dismissively. 'I can do whatever I like in the meantime.'

'Not if there's a risk that you could be pregnant by me,' Raffaele bit out wrathfully. 'At the very least that should've kept you away from other men!'

Vivi's eyes lit up with violet flames of anger because she could not credit that he could believe he had any rights over her. At the same time, she was struggling against an almost overwhelming need to stare at him and drink in his visual presence like an addictive drug. And the awareness of those conflicting urges only infuriated her more and made her tongue sharper.

'Nothing would keep me away from other men, least of all a very *unlikely* possibility of that sort!' she challenged back with ringing emphasis. 'You don't own me, Raffaele, so don't behave as though you do!'

'That is not how I am behaving,' Raffaele proclaimed with a raw edge to his accented drawl, his lean, darkly handsome features set hard as granite. 'You're not in a position to be with anyone else right now.'

'And how do you make that out?' Vivi prompted very drily, aware of his fury because the very atmosphere was smouldering with his tension. His eyes were bright as gilded metal, his sculpted bone structure rigid. Yet on some level she wanted to move closer and smooth her fingertips over the rigidity of his shapely mouth, breathe in the scent of his skin, *feel* the heat of him. But how could she still want such things from him? After all that had happened between them, how *could* he still make her feel that way? It reminded her that her only real defence with Raffaele was to keep him at a safe distance and if that made him angry, so be it.

'Do I really need to spell it out?'

'I think you do because I'm not getting it,' Vivi admitted shakily. 'I can't see why anything that I do should be your business either before *or* after this stupid wedding. It's not as though we're in a relationship.'

'*Che diavolo!*' he intoned with suppressed savagery, stalking across the small room like a volcano threaten-

ing to erupt. 'If you do prove to be pregnant, am I supposed to take your word for it that you have not been
with another man since you were with me?'

Those harsh words slammed into Vivi like bricks.
Loathing and anger engulfed her in a heady wave. He
thought she had gone from sleeping with him to sleeping with another man that fast? That she was such a
treacherous slut that she couldn't even be trusted to act
in a fair and decent way? Incredulous at the insult, Vivi
walked out to the front door.

'What are you doing?' Raffaele demanded.

White with anger, Vivi yanked open the door. 'Waiting for you to leave.'

'I'm not.'

'Either you leave or I call the police and have you
removed,' Vivi warned him fiercely. 'You're a hateful,
arrogant, insensitive man and I refuse to have anything
more to do with you! Get out!'

'I spoke only the truth. I said out loud what any man
would've been thinking,' Raffaele argued succinctly in
his own defence.

'Out!' Vivi exclaimed breathlessly. 'How dare you
insult me? How dare you suggest that I would go from
making that mistake with you to making it with someone else as well? Who the heck do you think you are?
And if you think I'm going to marry you now, you've
got another thought coming!'

'Vivi,' Raffaele breathed in a driven undertone, staring down at her, willing her to calm down, but her vi-
brant face was frozen and her eyes were as luminous
with temper as distant stars.

'Go!' Vivi snapped impatiently.

Raffaele left, colour mantling his high cheekbones, a huge sense of angry dissatisfaction gripping him. He had wanted to know who the boyfriend was, how long she had been seeing him, where they had spent the evening. But, inexplicably, he had asked none of those questions. Why? His brain had zeroed in on the suspicion that she had now become intimate with the other man and he hadn't been able to think beyond that disturbing level. Apart from the putative possibility of a pregnancy and the lines that would be blurred if she was also having sex with someone else, why had he got so angry?

He couldn't possibly be jealous. He didn't have a jealous bone in his entire body, had never once experienced that unpleasant emotion. He stayed in control of his emotions, rose above the negative aspects and refused to give them ground, he reminded himself stubbornly. But he had lost the detachment he valued so highly and had contrived to offend Vivi into threatening not to marry him, after all. She didn't mean it, of course, he told himself doggedly, of course she didn't mean it. Nobody got so mad that they burned their boats while still sitting in them, not even Vivi could be that foolish…

The next morning, Vivi was packing a travelling bag when Zoe appeared in the doorway. 'You had a fight with him last night,' she muttered, wide-eyed with consternation. 'You told him you weren't going to marry him, after all.'

'And he didn't *listen*!' Vivi hissed back between fu-

riously gritted teeth. 'Raffaele doesn't listen to what
he doesn't want to hear. Well, he'll soon find out that *I*
mean what I say.'

'Where are you going?'

'I'm going down to John and Liz for a few days. I
need a break and I've got some holiday time to use. If I
hurry I can catch the early train,' she pointed out, looking at her younger sister with belated concern. 'Will you
be all right here on your own for a while?'

'Of course,' Zoe assured her, gently removing a top
from Vivi's crushing grip to shake it out and fold it
neatly before slotting it into the bag for her enraged
sibling. 'If you don't marry him, where does that leave
John and Liz?'

Vivi swallowed hard, thinking it took Zoe to voice
that leading question and paling as the consequences of
her angry refusal formed in front of her. 'I don't know.
I'll work something out,' she swore.

Raffaele had always prided himself on his nerves of
steel but when Vivi extended her leave and stayed missing right up until forty-eight hours before the wedding,
he was desperate enough to visit her sister again and
ask if *she* knew where she was.

'Our foster parents' place,' Zoe revealed. 'I assumed
you must know.'

Raffaele clenched his teeth, got the address and organised a helicopter. He didn't know what he was planning to say to Vivi. He toyed with the idea of telling
her the truth about that dossier on Arianna but who
could tell what would happen if he opened that can of

worms? Would she even care about the threat to her former friend's happiness? Would that revelation cause trouble between her and her grandfather? And if it did cause trouble, how might that rebound on Raffaele and Arianna when he could not picture the older man backing down? He had no answers to those questions and decided he would have to work out his strategy according to what he learned when he got there.

That particular morning was a very trying one for Vivi. She had spent ten days with her foster parents in the familiar hurly-burly whirl of life at the old farmhouse. Not much had changed there. There was still a queue for the single bathroom every morning, noisily knocked doors, raised voices, shouts, squabbles and the thunder of noisy impatient feet on the stairs. Only when she heard John drive off with a carload of teenagers to do the school run did she emerge from the attic room where she had been staying. When she crept into the now vacant bathroom, she could hear Liz clattering round downstairs while she tidied up the kitchen and Vivi's heart was in her mouth as she opened the pregnancy testing kit she had bought the day before.

She was late and she had never been late before, her cycle usually being as regular as clockwork. Furthermore, the signs she had assumed were signalling the arrival of her period had intensified without the expected event arriving. She had waited and waited, hoped and prayed but the sensitivity of her breasts, the occasional bouts of nausea and the other unusual changes troubling her had persisted.

It couldn't be, it simply couldn't be, she was thinking as she performed the test with shaking hands and sat down to wait for the result. It couldn't possibly happen with Raffaele di Mancini, whom she hated…could it? No, fate couldn't be that cruel. Her hands coiled together tight and squeezed hard. She had had sex with him without precautions. Logic warned her that she deserved whatever she got from that ill-judged encounter. It was not as though she were stupid, it was not as though she hadn't known the risk as well as any other young woman. Unhappily, common sense hadn't featured in that episode and now she was appreciating that passion was even more dangerous than she had thought and that uncontrolled passion in that particular field could mean life-changing consequences.

Overhead she heard the irritating thwack-thwack of a helicopter and she winced, her head aching from a troubled night of sleep. Ironically she had fled to what had once been her home in search of peace only to discover that peace wasn't available to her anywhere because she could not run away from the repercussions of her angry decision not to marry Raffaele. Even now, at this late stage, she was listing them…the loss of Liz and John's home, not to mention the upheaval that would cause for the children dependent on them, whose security would be torn away.

And she knew the cost of that, she knew the cost of constantly changing foster homes better than anyone, she reminded herself in anguish. Then there would be the jobs lost at Hacketts Tech, the devastation that would engulf so many lives. And her grandfather would probably never forgive her for her defiance, not that she craved his good opinion and affection *that* much. In short, she had reached the conclusion that only a totally selfish cow would refuse to marry Raffaele in such circumstances. In temper, she had dug herself into a corner and now she didn't like herself very much.

Emerging from that despairing flood of reflections, Vivi belatedly recalled the pregnancy test and checked her watch before standing up to check the result. And the result sent a wave of dizziness currenting through her like a stinging electric charge. Dry-mouthed, she read the positive result and tottered down onto the edge of the bath because she didn't think her legs would hold her up any longer.

Panic filled her. A baby…*her* as a mother with a baby. That alien concept shattered what remained of her composure. She squeezed her eyes tight shut and scanned the result again but it didn't change. She thought of her little nephew, Teddy, and her tense face softened because she adored her sister's little boy. Were she to have a Teddy or a female equivalent of Teddy, she would love her baby, protect and nurture her child. She had a big heart and plenty of love to offer even though she couldn't currently see a way through the practical difficulties lying ahead. But should she even be considering bringing this child into the world when the world offered other more convenient options?

But no, she could not face a termination because she believed she would be haunted for ever by such a choice. Teddy would not have existed had Winnie chosen that route and the idea that she might never have had the opportunity to know her little nephew appalled

Vivi. No, she would have her baby, whatever the consequences, not least her foster parents' disappointment that she could have been so irresponsible, her grandfather's rage and her sisters' distress that she had refused to do what she was supposed to do.

'Vivi!' Liz shouted up from the ground floor.

Wondering how long she had been sitting in a daze contemplating her radically altered future, Vivi stood up and disposed of the evidence of the pregnancy test before going downstairs into the kitchen, where she stopped dead, frozen into shock at the sight of Raffaele sitting at the table with a cup of coffee.

'Vivi…you have a visitor,' Liz Brooke greeted her with a smile. 'I wish you'd told us what was going on.'

'Going on?' Vivi queried in bewilderment.

'That you were supposed to be getting married the day after tomorrow but that you and Raffaele had a terrible row and you broke it off,' Liz supplied ruefully. 'I knew you were unhappy but I also knew that when you were ready to talk, you would let me know what was bothering you.'

Caught on the hop by the startling revelation that Raffaele had broken the story of the wedding to her foster mother, Vivi stiffened even more. What on earth was he doing here? How the heck had he even found out where she was staying?

Unaffected by either her dismay or self-consciousness, Raffaele slid fluidly upright, brilliant dark golden eyes welded to Vivi. In jeans, ankle boots and a long-sleeved green top, she was casually clad and bare of make-up. Her corkscrew curls were caught up at the back of her small head in a clasp, stray tendrils curling colourfully round her pale heart-shaped face. Her beautiful blue eyes were shadowed, the faint scattering of freckles across her nose starkly defined by her pallor, her soft mouth taut.

'I'm hoping you'll talk to me now that you've had a chance to think things over,' he murmured softly.

A heady combination of self-loathing and regret attacked Vivi and her eyes prickled with tears, making her blink rapidly. What an awful mess she had made of her life! Raffaele di Mancini was the father of her unborn child and, not only did he not love her, he also didn't care about her in the slightest. She was ashamed of that reality.

Two years ago, she had started out with a crush on Raffaele that had ended with her hating him. She wasn't very good at dealing with losing people she cared about or rejection, she acknowledged sickly. She had missed the loving arms of her parents even though she had been too young to recall their actual faces once they had gone. There had also been foster homes that were great that she had been moved on from, leaving her wondering constantly if there was something bad about her that people didn't like and hammering what little confidence she'd still retained.

Raffaele's reappearance in her life had awakened all sorts of conflicting emotions because when he had turned his back on her after that scandal, he had *hurt* her. And Vivi always remembered pain more easily than pleasure. Her self-esteem had been destroyed once she'd realised that the man she was falling in love with had readily believed that she was a prostitute. Time and time again she had dissected her own behaviour with him, asking herself what she had done or said wrong to give him such a false impression of her.

'Some breakfast, Vivi?' Liz prompted.

'No, thanks.' The thought of food made Vivi feel nauseous while she tried to prevent herself from staring at Raffaele, all sleek and dark and sensationally handsome in a business suit that would have looked more at home in a fancy office than in her foster parents' battered old kitchen. Her chest tightened, her ribcage striving to expand to draw in breath. Her mouth was dry as a bone. 'I'll make myself some tea,' she said, desperate to occupy herself.

'No, let me,' Liz overruled, switching on the kettle. 'Evidently you two have a lot to talk about.'

Yes, they did, Vivi acknowledged with a sinking sensation, thinking of the child she had conceived. Much as she might want to, she couldn't conceal that from him. All sorts of complications had arisen from Winnie's decision not to tell the father of her child that she was pregnant and Vivi was determined not to make the same mistake. Evading Raffaele's questioning gaze, she grasped the mug of tea that Liz extended to her.

'Let's go out into the garden while it's still sunny,' she urged tautly.

CHAPTER SIX

'I CAN'T BELIEVE you told Liz about the wedding,' Vivi admitted, sinking down on the home-made seat below the flowering cherry tree where she had once spent her most peaceful hours.

'I can't believe that you *didn't*,' Raffaele traded. 'Were you hoping it would all just go away if you vanished?'

Vivi flushed miserably and set her teeth squarely together. She wasn't proud of her behaviour but the whole situation had simply become overwhelming. Finding herself trapped between her grandfather's demands and Raffaele's, not to mention the demands of her own conscience and her sisters' expectations, she had buried her head in the sand about the potential consequences and fled.

'All the arrangements are still in place,' Raffaele informed her quietly.

'I can't believe that you would still want to go ahead after what you said to me the last time I saw you!' Vivi countered tartly.

'I'm guilty of creating this situation by not maintaining a more businesslike relationship with you,' Raffaele breathed in a driven undertone, a faint edge of dark colour accentuating his exotic cheekbones. 'I blurred the lines between us, brought down the boundaries. What I said to you *was* offensive and my only excuse is that I became angry at the idea of you being with another man.'

'I broke things off with Jude that night,' Vivi muttered wearily, letting her luminous blue eyes linger on his strong dark face to appreciate his classic bone structure. 'I told him that I'd met someone else and even though he was generous about it, it was a very uncomfortable couple of hours.'

Raffaele stared down at her where she sat, slender thighs outlined by tight denim, delicate breasts defined by her stretchy top. On edge, conscious of the thrumming pulse kicking off at his groin, he lifted his gaze up only to linger on the ripe full curve of her mouth instead and his brain, which usually lacked imagination, suddenly flashed up a fantasy image that sent an unbearable stab of hunger coursing through his lean, powerful body. He swung away and walked over to the low hedge that divided the garden from the field beyond.

'This isn't a working farm any more, is it?' he remarked tightly, wondering what it was about her that aroused him to feats of fantasy he had always believed lay far beyond the reaches of his logical mind.

'No. Liz's grandparents were the last generation of farmers. The land was sold off before she was born. Her husband, John, is a plumber and he set up a business here. It went well and then he had a stroke and everything fell apart until he had recovered enough to work again,' she told him ruefully, thinking that that was where her foster parents' problems had begun—with ill health and the subsequent reduction of their income. Through no fault of their own they had fallen behind with their mortgage.

Vivi heaved a sigh and stared stonily down at her clasped hands. Tell him, her inner voice urged, *tell him* and get it over with! But why wasn't he giving her the opening she had expected? What about the doctor's appointment that had never taken place? Wasn't he still concerned about the risk of conception? Or were women more inclined to worry about such things? Or, more probably, was his omission a sign that he had never really expected anything to come from their unwise encounter? After all, hadn't he already expressed his regrets on that score? Declaring that it never should have happened? That they should have maintained a businesslike relationship? Her mind boggled at that concept. Businesslike? *Really?*

'How did you find out where I was?' she asked baldly.

'I dug it out of Zoe,' Raffaele admitted. 'But she only told me to get rid of me.'

'I hope you didn't upset her!' Vivi snapped.

'No. She asked me if I thought I could bring you home and admitted that she missed you.'

'And what did you say?' Vivi pressed.

'That I intended to try…what else?' Raffaele shrugged a broad shoulder in graceful dismissal.

Vivi swallowed hard, mentally searching for the right words with which to make her announcement until it dawned on her that there *were* no right words, no magical way of making what he couldn't possibly want to hear more palatable. 'I might as well tell you and get it over with,' she framed stiffly. 'I'm pregnant.'

Raffaele swung back to her, dark eyes, shaded to the colour of melted caramel, widening, a faint frown line etching between his ebony brows as if he wasn't quite sure he had heard her correctly.

'I'm pregnant,' Vivi said again, shattering the sudden silence that had fallen. 'I waited until today to do the test because I wanted to be absolutely sure of the result.'

'There is no room for error?' Raffaele's spectacular bone structure had pulled taut below his bronzed skin, the smooth planes of his hard cheekbones prominent.

'None whatsoever,' she whispered, intimidated by his lack of comment.

A baby? Momentarily, Raffaele felt as though he had been gut-punched and he compressed his lips because he wasn't ready to be a father. He had naively assumed it wouldn't happen, that the same golden strand of luck that had eased his path since birth would hold true. And it *hadn't*, which was a major shock to his system. Vivi was pregnant with his son or daughter, years before he had planned such an event would take place. The concept shook him badly because nobody was more conscious than him that a child was a permanent feature in one's life, not something that could be shuffled aside while he focused on his goals and taken up again at a more convenient date. Even more pertinently, he had planned to handpick the future mother of his children, had even mentally prepared a brief checklist of the kind of woman he would choose because in his private life he was highly averse to risk. And Vivi screamed risk on every sane level…

'Raffaele?' Vivi almost whispered in the lingering silence.

But while Vivi emanated dangerous vibes, she also excited the hell out of him and, *Dio mio*, she was an incredible beauty, Raffaele savoured, studying her with shimmering dark golden eyes while pitching his careful checklist of desirable maternal and wifely attributes into a mental drawer to be buried deep and forgotten. *Prima di agire pensaci*…look before you leap had been one of his father's favourite sayings and Raffaele was supremely aware that he had neither looked nor considered consequences in anything he had *ever* done with Vivi. And yet, bafflingly, everything with her always felt seductively, inexplicably natural.

'At the very least, my child will have my name when you marry me the day after tomorrow,' Raffaele breathed, kicking his brain back into gear to assume that that was one obstacle already cleared.

Vivi's soft mouth opened and closed again and she bent her head, her brain buzzing with thoughts. 'Is that really all you've got to say right now?' she queried helplessly. 'I haven't got a recording device playing. You're not in a court of law either. You can be honest about your feelings.'

Raffaele's lush black lashes dipped low over his glittering gaze. 'Honesty can be a much-overrated trait. I am shocked, but I am also very much of a practical nature. A child changes everything. Even you must acknowledge that.'

'*Even*…me? Do you really think that I am that irresponsible?'

His shapely mouth quirked. 'Perhaps not irresponsible but you do like to defy conventional expectations.'

A tiny bit of her hostility drained away. 'Yes. My child will be as proud to have *my* name as yours but I don't see how marriage—'

Raffaele shifted a fluid brown hand to cut in. 'A child's needs and rights are best protected within the law. We have to be married for our child to inherit my estate without challenge.'

Vivi frowned. 'And that's important to you?'

Raffaele gritted his teeth. 'Some day it will be important to our child as well.'

Vivi studied him in near wonderment because he was so deadly serious. She told him that she was pregnant and Raffaele's brain zeroed straight to matrimonial law and their child's inheritance rights, leapfrogging over more immediately pressing matters. 'Money isn't everything,' she said quietly.

'It is a much more complex question than that and you know it,' Raffaele parried. 'Obviously we will go ahead and marry now because to do anything else would be foolish in the extreme.'

Vivi pondered that controversial statement and shifted uncomfortably in her seat. At that moment it seemed to her that every pressure that could be brought to bear on her to marry Raffaele was weighing her down and shredding her every argument. 'I wasn't expecting this attitude from you,' she admitted in a rush. 'I thought you would be furious.'

'What right would I have to be furious?' Raffaele incised. 'We took the same risk together. Why would we waste our time now lamenting the outcome?'

His outlook was, as he had warned her, innately practical. Parting her lips uncertainly, Vivi said, 'I could've considered a termination.'

'Which I would undoubtedly never have known about. But you did *not* choose that path. Instead you are telling me openly and honestly and I am grateful for that,' Raffaele intoned tautly. 'This is something we must share.'

'Yes,' Vivi acknowledged, dropping her copper head, the slender column of her neck below her ponytail looking disconcertingly vulnerable to his wary gaze. 'I couldn't entertain a termination after getting to know and love my sister's little boy, Teddy. I don't think I could give a child up for adoption either. But I *still* can't imagine becoming a mother...'

'I would say the same about becoming a father, except that in many ways for the past decade I have acted as Arianna's father,' Raffaele admitted in a rueful undertone. 'I was a twenty-year-old student when her mother died. Arianna was twelve and in boarding school. I'm ashamed to say that I initially tried to avoid the responsibility, leaving her to spend her holidays with schoolfriends and ignoring her need to have a settled home.'

'So, what changed?'

Raffaele looked pained. 'She sent me a letter asking me why I didn't like her because, according to her, if you like someone, you want to *see* that person. I was ashamed. I had always thought of her as my unpleasant stepmother's child, *not* as my father's daughter, *not* as my half-sister, and even with both our parents dead I had gone on looking at her in that light. She was lonely and unhappy at school and I was her only close relative. I had to man up fast but the lesson stayed with me. Wishing things could be different doesn't change facts. It's better to face trouble head-on.'

A glimmer of rueful amusement lightened Vivi's eyes and her head lifted. 'Is that what I am? Trouble?'

'From the very first moment I saw you and wanted you,' Raffaele confirmed without hesitation. 'You were my sister's friend and that alone should've restrained me.'

Faint colour warmed her pale cheeks. 'Together we're not very good at restraint.'

Raffaele gazed back at her, the pulse of desire thrumming through his lean, powerful frame, tensing his muscles and accelerating his heartbeat.

Her gaze colliding with those dark golden eyes, damp heat seemed to coat her entire skin surface, her nipples snapping taut, her mouth running dry. She tore her attention from him but still he lingered in her mind's eye, sleek and dark and beautiful with a sensuality that burned and made her ache unbearably. She swallowed hard on that grudging acknowledgement and suppressed it even quicker because they had far more important questions to consider and she was mortified by her lack of mental discipline.

'So, we let the wedding go ahead because I'm pregnant and you think it's safer for our child to be born legitimate with regard to the law and all that sort of thing,' she concluded in a weary surge.

'And because I believe that you should have my support throughout your pregnancy.'

Vivi's eyes opened wide and violet disbelief darkened them as she glanced back at him again. '*Throughout?* Look, I'm prepared to go through with the wedding but I don't want anything to do with you beyond that!'

'That's no longer an achievable objective when you're carrying my baby,' Raffaele spelt out with finality.

'Oh, yes, it is!' Vivi argued vehemently. 'I don't need you for support while I'm pregnant.'

'But I want to *be* there for you,' Raffaele countered levelly.

'Oh, stop being so pious!' Vivi flashed back at him as she sprang to her feet in passionate annoyance. 'Maybe you think you're saying what I want to hear! Or maybe you think I couldn't cope without you! Or maybe even you simply suffer from an over-developed conscience! But you don't ever get to attach strings to me just because you knocked me up!'

Raffaele grimaced. 'Don't be crude.'

Vivi tossed her head, copper hair glinting like polished metal in the sunshine, her triangular face flushed and glowing with resentment as she hurriedly turned away from him. What a nightmare she would be storing up for the future if she allowed herself to become dependent on a guy who had no feelings for her other than those of obligation! If she wasn't careful, she might start getting attached to him again, she thought fearfully. Heaven knew she could already hardly keep her hands off him and what more might result from such a powerful attraction? 'You get to attach strings to the baby after it's born, *not* to me.'

'While you are carrying my child I have a duty of care towards you both,' Raffaele contradicted drily. 'A desire to be supportive is not attaching strings. I want you to agree to stay married to me and live with me until our child is born, at least.'

Vivi took an outraged step back from him. 'Absolutely not! Are you crazy? Our agreement was that we go through with the ceremony and then go our separate ways!'

Raffaele groaned out loud in frustration. 'And now we have something much more important to factor into that calculation…our baby,' he reminded her. 'Nothing is the same now. Our priorities have to change.'

'Well, they *have* changed,' Vivi proclaimed defensively, angry that he was unappreciative of the sacrifice she was already making and indeed was now demanding even more from her. Here she was struggling to hold him at arm's length and minimise their interaction while he was demanding that she expose herself to much more. 'Obviously I'm willing to agree to go ahead with the wedding without any further argument but that doesn't mean I'm willing to sacrifice my freedom for the whole of my pregnancy.'

'What vital freedom will you have if you live separately from me?' Raffaele demanded. 'Are you planning to continue drinking and dating while pregnant? Is that the freedom that you fear losing?'

'Oh, for goodness' sake, Raffaele, I haven't even thought about stuff like that!' Vivi fired back at him in exasperation. 'I won't be doing anything against medical guidelines, and right at this minute dating has about as much appeal for me as plunging into an ice pool! But on the other hand, living with you when you're so arrogant and judgemental and domineering has even less appeal!'

Raffaele, unaccustomed to criticism and prepared from the teenage years to see himself as a very eligible partner, released his breath in a controlled hiss. 'What will you do when you don't feel well? Surely there will be such times? Who will you lean on then? Who will look after you?'

Vivi gritted her teeth. 'I don't need looking after and I don't *lean* on people for support!' she fielded with distaste and a proud toss of her head.

Raffaele stood poised and cool and resolute, impervious to the wash of her angry denial of vulnerability. 'But you may need to over the next few months and surely it is better to lean on me than on others?'

Vivi paled at that unwelcome point, thinking of how under par Winnie had been in the initial months of her pregnancy while simultaneously recognising in dismay how her grandad might react to news of her condition. Disapproving as he had been of her sister being a single parent, he would not be pleased even though Vivi would be legally married before her child was born.

Furthermore, the idea of having to approach the older man for any form of help, financial or otherwise, during her pregnancy was equally off-putting and would decimate her pride. She would have to put her money where her mouth was, as the saying went, and manage on her own. Accepting Raffaele's support might be an unpalatable concept but as he was as responsible for the child she carried as she was, it would hurt her pride less.

Raffaele scrutinised her tense stance and wondered if anyone had ever resisted him to such a degree. It annoyed the hell out of him that she refused to see common sense, that she was determined to deny the obvious benefits of remaining his wife while she was pregnant. Shouldn't she want that security and support? Her slight frame was drooping a little and it crossed his mind that she was not only tired but also very slender.

Healthily slender? It seemed to him that she had lost weight. Had she been worrying too much to take time out to care for herself? Of course, she had been worrying, he told himself impatiently. Hadn't he threatened redundancies at her place of work? He had put a lot of pressure on her quite deliberately. Was it any wonder that she should now struggle to see him as a potentially supportive partner with whom she could share her pregnancy?

'You don't trust me,' Raffaele murmured grimly.

'Oh, don't be offended!' Vivi urged with an embarrassed gesture of dismissal. 'I don't trust anyone but my sisters and John and Liz. It's safer that way and you don't get disappointed or...*hurt*.'

Raffaele reached for her knotted fists and slowly smoothed out the tension in her thin fingers. 'I will not disappoint or hurt you. I will look after you to the best of my ability and once the baby is born you will have your freedom back.'

Vivi glanced up involuntarily and collided with dark golden eyes. Her colour heightened, a knot tightening in her throat. She swallowed convulsively, her eyes prickling. His hands over hers were soothing but he was her enemy and she would be foolish to forget that for a second. Nor could he possibly appreciate that if she lost control of her feelings for him again he was very likely to hurt her. 'I feel like bursting into tears,' she confided chokily. 'And I don't know why. Think it might be pregnancy hormones or something.'

'Maybe so. I'll feel better once you've had a doctor check you over,' Raffaele admitted tautly.

'I'm so tired,' she whispered unevenly. 'I'm so tired I could go to sleep standing up.'

'Stress,' Raffaele framed, hoping she didn't choose that moment to remind him that *he* had put her under that stress. 'I have to fight for what's right, *bella mia*.'

'But I don't agree with you,' she muttered ruefully.

'You never agree with anything I say,' Raffaele countered with sardonic amusement. 'But right now, all I want to do is whisk you home to London and ensure that you consult a doctor. Is that acceptable?'

Just at that moment the image of her own comfortable bed had immense appeal and she nodded grudgingly, uncertain that she wanted to see a doctor as yet but reckoning that it couldn't do any actual harm to be clued up on what lay ahead, even if her sister's experiences had already warned her of most of the physical pitfalls.

'And while we're with your foster mother, we'll work out some way of getting her and your foster father to London for the wedding,' Raffaele concluded with assurance.

'It won't work. They've got too many responsibilities on the home front with the kids.'

'Somehow we'll make it work,' Raffaele proclaimed with immoveable assurance.

And Vivi wondered what it said about her that even when Raffaele was endeavouring to be decent, she wanted to slap him. She bit her tongue, compressed her lips and said nothing and reckoned that that was possibly the best way of dealing with him.

CHAPTER SEVEN

'IT DOESN'T LOOK too tight?' Vivi pressed anxiously, sucking in her breath and turning this way and that in front of the full-length mirror to check her reflection.

Her sister looked nervous, stressed, not her usual cool, snippety self, Winnie acknowledged worriedly, crossing the room to pour her sister a drink and give her some Dutch courage. That was the joy of them all having spent the previous night in their grandfather's grandiose split-level London apartment. Every room came equipped with more extras than an exclusive hotel.

'It's a figure-hugging dress,' Winnie pointed out. 'It's supposed to be a good fit.'

'But she had to have the seams let out yesterday because it was too tight over the bust in the final fitting.' Zoe chuckled from across the room. 'The designer was aghast. I mean, who puts on that much weight *there* of all places?'

'Yes,' Vivi muttered. 'She was distinctly irritated behind the understanding smiles.'

Winnie thrust a glass of spirit into her sister's hand. 'Here, drown your sorrows,' she advised. 'Obviously you've been comfort-eating. You shouldn't be letting all this get to you to that extent.'

'It got to you as well,' Vivi reminded her elder sibling.

'Yes, but I had to stay on after the wedding because Eros still had Teddy. You're not required to stay beyond the reception today,' Winnie pointed out breezily.

Vivi paled and abstractedly tipped the glass to her lips and then *remembered* what she couldn't forget for even as long as two minutes and she hurriedly set the glass down again, her nerves twisting in a climbing spiral of tension. Her boobs ached in the tight confines of the corseting beneath her dress. Never before had she sported such generous curves. All part of the process of change taking place in her body, the nurse at the swanky medical practice Raffaele had taken her to the day before had told her cheerfully. Vivi didn't feel quite so cheerful about those changes, which were happening sooner than she had expected.

'You know, that *is* a truly fabulous dress.' Zoe sighed appreciatively, studying her sister's lithe and slender silhouette in the off-the-shoulder gown fashioned from rich gold lace sprinkled with shimmering embroidery. 'That colour against your hair is breathtaking. Quite the fashion statement too.'

'Teamed with the tiara and the diamonds that Raffaele sent you yesterday, you look like a queen,' Winnie murmured with an amused smile. 'Very dignified, very elegant.'

'Yeah,' Vivi muttered, scrutinising the platinum and diamond tiara anchored in her upswept hair, not to mention the diamond necklace and the drop earrings. 'I don't know what Raffaele was thinking of offering me such expensive jewellery to wear. I don't feel entitled to wear his family stuff.'

'He has close relatives attending today,' Winnie reminded her wryly. 'He's having to make this show look more real than it is for their benefit and I suppose the bride wearing the family heirlooms is part of that.'

Close relatives... Arianna would be attending for sure, Vivi reckoned absently. How would *she* behave? She couldn't imagine Arianna being nasty and she herself was willing to let bygones be bygones this long after the scandal that had separated them.

'This all feels real enough to *me*,' Vivi confided in a brittle voice, her tension climbing even higher at the prospect of walking down the aisle to Raffaele on her grandfather's arm in front of so many people, because she was only now appreciating that it was going to be a *very* big society wedding. She had paid no heed to the actual wedding arrangements. They had been left in her grandfather's hands while she continued to act as though none of it were anything to do with her because she had still been desperately looking for an escape route. In any case, why would she have had preferences or opinions to express about a wedding that was a virtual fake?

Unfortunately, that false bravado had deserted her the night before while she and her sisters and Winnie's husband had dined with their grandad. Stamboulas Fotakis had been downright ecstatic about the number of wedding invitations he had had to send out and the very high number of acceptances that had come in. He was equally delighted that so many titled society figures were keen to attend *his* granddaughter's wedding and he had unashamedly rejoiced in the bridegroom's pedigreed connections.

Listening to that uninhibited enthusiasm, Vivi had finally understood the older man's eagerness to marry his grandchildren off to men of high social standing. Their grandfather was a self-made man from a very poor background and grand social connections clearly meant a great deal to him. Luckily for them all, however, no media outlet had yet connected the bride, Vivi Fox, with Vivi Mardas, once slated in the tabloids.

Winnie squeezed Vivi's hand in a comforting gesture and then winced and frowned. 'Your fingers are as cold as ice... Where did you put that drink? You need to warm up.'

Glancing around, Winnie spotted the glass that Vivi had abandoned and retrieved it to extend it to her again.

'I can't,' Vivi muttered tightly.

'I can think of only one reason why you wouldn't take one little drink,' Winnie said with a frown of bewilderment. 'And that's not possible.'

'I'm afraid it is. I'm pregnant.' Vivi almost whispered the confession, grateful to have finally got the announcement out.

'You can't be,' Winnie assured her confidently.

Zoe was quicker on the uptake and more informed. 'That night you spent at Raffaele's house?' she queried wide-eyed. 'You actually *slept* with him? But you said you had had too much to drink.'

'Well, I wasn't going to admit *that* to you, was I?' Vivi fielded, her cheeks a feverish pink as she lifted her head defiantly high.

'Oh, my goodness, Vivi!' Winnie collapsed down on the edge of the bed while staring at her copper-haired sibling with wide dismayed eyes. 'You're expecting a baby? *Seriously?*'

'Yes,' Vivi confirmed flatly. 'And I won't be coming home after the reception either. Raffaele is obsessed with his belief that it's his duty to look after me while I'm pregnant, so I've agreed to stay with him until the baby is born.'

'But you hate him,' Zoe murmured in disbelief.

'He has his moments,' Vivi muttered repressively.

'Obviously,' Winnie pronounced witheringly. 'When are you planning to share this particular piece of good news with Grandad?'

'Be my guest and do it for me. I'll only have a massive row with him, which is a bit pointless when, essentially, I will have kept to my side of the deal and gone through with the wedding he demanded,' Vivi pointed out ruefully. 'It's all *his* fault anyway.'

'And how do you make that out?' Winnie prompted.

'Well, if Grandad hadn't forced me into seeing Raffaele again and spending time with him, this would never have happened,' Vivi declared, struggling to justify her fall from grace any way she could.

'Do you find Raffaele *that* irresistible?' Winnie asked curiously.

Vivi shrugged, refusing to be drawn on that score, but her face was burning.

'It says something in Raffaele's favour that he's willing to take responsibility for the baby and that he's so keen to look after both of you,' Zoe commented thoughtfully.

Vivi squared her slim shoulders. 'I don't need anyone looking after me.'

'And yet somehow you've agreed to let *him* do it,' Winnie remarked with a suggestive roll of her eyes just as a knock sounded on the door. 'I think that's our cue to leave for the church.'

The instant he heard the low buzz of comment spreading through the big church, Raffaele knew that the bride had arrived and he swung round to steal a look.

'Porca miseria,' he intoned in astonished appreciation because Vivi looked stunning in that gown. She had not even kept him waiting as he had expected, arriving bang on time, typically contriving that Vivi trademark of surprising him. She was a dazzling figure sheathed in gold lace that enhanced her porcelain skin and copper hair, while the legendary di Mancini diamonds glittered on her proud head and at her slender throat and delicate ears as befitted his bride. He seriously doubted, however, that any previous bride in his family history had enjoyed quite her level of beauty. His chest swelled with pride. No, nobody looking at Vivi's exquisite face and shape would be surprised by his sudden impetuous marriage. Stronger men than him would've succumbed to such undeniable allure, Raffaele conceded, fighting the throb of arousal threatening at his groin.

His keen gaze mercilessly sliced away the sight of

Stamboulas Fotakis beaming by the bride's side and his handsome mouth compressed into a hard line. The old man would pay dearly for his mistake in having threatened Raffaele's family. Raffaele had already fine-tuned the punishment and put it in place like bait, secure in the knowledge that Stam invariably went for a certain type of deal. Stam would not enjoy being burned and he would learn not to cross Raffaele again. Raffaele would've gone for an infinitely more ruthless penalty had it not occurred to him that Vivi's child, *his* child, would be Stam's great-grandchild, which now qualified the callous old codger as family. And today was also obviously the day when he would retrieve that dangerous dossier on Arianna and that threat would be suppressed for all time.

In short, Raffaele was in a surprisingly upbeat mood for a man who had been forced to the altar. By the end of the year he would be a father and well on the way to becoming a divorced and single man again as well. That was definitely worth celebrating, wasn't it? He would be gaining an heir without the encumbrance of a wife and he would have no good reason to remarry. He would've done his duty by continuing the family line yet he would also be reclaiming his freedom to live life exactly as he liked. It wasn't quite how he had planned his future but the key to success was often flexibility and he was convinced that he could make that change in plans work.

Even so, little apprehensions like pieces of grit niggled beneath his skin. How would Vivi cope as a wealthy single parent? Would their child suffer from seeing less of his or her father? Wouldn't it bother him when Vivi remarried and his child gained a step-parent? There was nothing surer than that a woman with Vivi's looks would not remain single and alone for very long. His own experience of having a step-parent had been unpleasant but then his father's drug-addled second wife had been a disaster in every way. There was no reason why Vivi shouldn't find an acceptable partner, capable of acting as a decent stepfather.

Yet the very thought of Vivi becoming intimate with another man or his child enjoying a stepfather's care slashed at Raffaele like a thousand cuts from a tiny, sharp-bladed knife because it felt wrong to him on every level. Not only would it be less than ideal, it wasn't what he wanted for his family and it wouldn't provide the lasting security that his son or his daughter deserved. But undoubtedly, unlike Vivi, he was too set in his ways, too conventional, too traditional and far too much of a perfectionist to cheerfully accept a less than perfect scenario. He would also be defying his father's belief that marriage was for life, but then his father's second marriage had not set a very good example. All of them would have been happier had there been a divorce. The conviction that in some circumstances divorce was the only practical option had removed most of Raffaele's objections to that solution.

Unaware that Raffaele was already planning their separation and divorce, Vivi spared not a glance at the packed pews that lined the aisle. Her attention leapt straight to Raffaele, lingering on his strong, devastatingly handsome features and the hard power and sensuality etched there that mirrored the lean grace of his tall, athletic body. In just a few months, she told herself urgently, she would be returning to her normal life. It didn't matter that just looking at Raffaele sent a curl of heat travelling up through her pelvis in a far from controlled and ladylike way. It didn't matter that this was not how she had expected her life to develop. As she should know better than anyone, life had a habit of throwing up surprises and her baby was one of them.

Raffaele was making an effort to be civil and she would make the same effort, she assured herself. They would be friends and she wouldn't fight with him any more. Her pregnancy would be peaceful and probably pretty boring but she would take boring over troubled any day of the week, she reasoned, striving to compose herself. The words of the marriage ceremony penetrated even though she was trying hard to block them out and then Raffaele took her hand and slid a platinum wedding ring on her finger, his fingers warm and sure on hers. But then Raffaele seemed to be sure of virtually everything he did, she brooded abstractedly; clearly he did not suffer from the same insecurities that often assailed her.

A little sliver of heat tingled in her pelvis as Raffaele spun her round to face him, dark golden eyes welding to her upturned face. Her knees went weak and wobbled and she fought the sensation fiercely. *Friends*, she reminded herself doggedly, friends who were going to get along like a house on fire for the next few months and behave like sensible adults. But he had such beautiful eyes, a little voice whispered deep in her brain, shimmering gold like melted caramel in sunshine, in an appraisal that banished the chilled knot of tension inside her.

'You look totally amazing in that dress, *bella mia*,' Raffaele breathed as his hand gripped hers to walk her down the aisle and the church organ swelled into a burst of triumphal music.

The spontaneous compliment warmed her cheeks and she stopped scolding herself for having noticed how arresting his eyes were. It wasn't his fault that he had lashes longer and thicker than many a woman would kill for, and it wasn't her fault that she was reacting to his stunning good looks either because that was simply hormones. Of course, that little sizzle of lingering attraction wasn't going to die off entirely, she reasoned, but it was nothing that she couldn't control. Being friends was going to work like a treat, she told herself.

Raffaele was reaching a far different conclusion because the gravity of the marriage ceremony had worked to remind him of every moral principle his father and his upbringing had instilled in him from an early age. Vivi was his wife and soon to be the mother of his child. To think of her as anything less, to dismiss her as merely a temporary aberration in his life was short-sighted and disrespectful to them both. At the very least he ought to give their marriage a chance…

After all, he *still* wanted her.

And on one level that awareness infuriated him because that had never happened to him before with a woman and it was more than a little unnerving. Usually sexual satisfaction led very quickly to lack of interest and boredom for Raffaele, turning his eyes in the direction of a new and more challenging quarry. But just at that moment, as he found his gaze clinging involuntarily to the neat fit of his bride's dress over the swell of her breasts and the pert curve of her bottom, Raffaele's high-voltage sex drive was wholly centred on Vivi and an instantaneous need to mark his territory smouldered like a banked-down fire inside him.

His long, brown fingers tightened on her wrist to turn her back to him and she blinked up at him in questioning surprise. A split second later, his mouth crushed hers in stormy demand. It wasn't a gentle kiss or a quiet formal acknowledgement of their new relationship; no, indeed, it was more a kiss of desire and possession and Vivi was utterly unprepared for it, particularly in front of an audience. Her heart thundered in her ears, her knees went from weak to numb and she leant helplessly against him for support, shaken by that passionate onslaught, for she would've sworn Raffaele was the last guy alive to treat her to a passionate kiss at the altar in front of hundreds of people, including the priest. It wasn't cool, it wasn't sophisticated but, my goodness, that uninhibited urgency was extraordinarily *hot*, she conceded helplessly, a slight involuntary shudder rippling through her as his tongue penetrated deep into the moist interior of her mouth and kicked off a surge of sensational response throughout her taut body.

Vivi was still shell-shocked by that sensual assault when he walked her back down the aisle. It wasn't what she had expected from a man as controlled and cool as Raffaele, indeed it had blown her every expectation of him out of the water, including their new cosy relationship as platonic friends patiently waiting out her unplanned pregnancy. In a daze she shook her head and encountered the smiling attention of a slender brunette. It was Arianna, her former friend and now her sister-in-law, she acknowledged, a wary smile softening her own lips.

Obviously, she would have to overlook the reality that Raffaele's sister had dumped her like a hot potato and turned her back on her two years earlier. The rejection had hurt, adding to the shamed sense of humiliation she had endured in the wake of the tabloid scandal, but it also struck her as completely unsurprising that Arianna would simply smile at her as if nothing had ever gone wrong between them. *That* was pure Arianna, warm and uncritical and, in truth, kind of naive about some things. Well, she didn't want to be at odds with the younger woman and if Arianna could accept her as her brother's wife, then surely she could be equally tolerant in accepting that for the present they were all part of the same family?

On the steps of the church, cameras and phones flashed in the direction of the newly married couple but Raffaele barely paused his steps, a strong arm curving to her taut spine to guide her towards the privacy of the limousine awaiting them. Vivi only managed a brief nod and smile towards her foster parents, John and Liz, who were standing in the crush with Zoe beside them, but she was impressed that Raffaele had kept his word and contrived to get them there and had done so without fuss.

'What did your grandfather say when you told him you were coming home with me after the wedding?' Raffaele prompted curiously as he swept her into the opulent car.

Vivi grimaced. 'I haven't told him yet,' she admitted wryly and, in receipt of an incredulous glance from Raffaele, she raised her own brows defensively. '*That* announcement would have kicked off a screaming row and I've had enough of those with Grandad. We don't agree on anything, so he doesn't know yet unless Winnie has told him. I asked my sisters to break the news. Winnie's more tactful than I am.'

Raffaele frowned. 'So, he doesn't know you're pregnant either,' he assumed, compressing his lips in disapproval.

'That wasn't something I wanted to get into with him face to face,' Vivi confided with a wince of discomfiture.

'He's going to be very much shocked when you leave for Italy with me,' Raffaele pointed out impatiently.

It was Vivi's turn to frown and she glanced at him uncertainly. 'But why would I be leaving for *Italy*?'

'I live there.'

'But you have a house here in London,' she pointed out in dismay.

'For business trips, visits. Obviously we will be living in my home in Italy,' Raffaele told her levelly. 'It would never have occurred to me that you expected to live anywhere else.'

Vivi's heart-shaped face had flushed. 'But I don't want to move to Italy!' she protested loudly.

'Tough,' Raffaele breathed, because as far as he was concerned it was non-negotiable. 'My bank is in Florence and my home is in Italy and I would like my child to be born there.'

'And that's that, is it?' Vivi hissed, blue eyes flaring violet with outraged resentment. 'Raffaele has spoken and I'm supposed to just fall into line?'

'It was more than a little impractical of you to assume that I would be content to live in London for the duration of your pregnancy.'

'I want my sisters with me… I want an English-speaking doctor!' Vivi blasted back at him shakily. 'It may surprise you but I've never had a baby before and I'm nervous.'

'Your eldest sister lives in Greece. Zoe is welcome to visit us whenever she likes, in fact she can move in with us if you want her to,' Raffaele proffered smoothly. 'The *palazzo* is vast and space is not a problem. I am also sure that I can find you English-speaking medical care but, of course, you may want to learn Italian.'

'Not right now, I don't!' Vivi flashed back at him.

'But you're not likely to spend the whole of your pregnancy in a bad temper,' Raffaele pointed out drily. 'I cannot be the only person who ever said no to you and that is my only crime.'

'Oh, stop trying to make me sound like a selfish cow or a spoilt child!' Vivi flung back impatiently. 'I've spent most of my life being told no and not getting what I want. I'm an old hand at settling for second best!'

Raffaele's remarkable dark golden eyes shimmered with reluctant amusement at the concept of his magnificent home or his very comfortable life in Italy being in any way second best. He was convinced that he could go a lifetime without ever meeting a second Vivi, with her eyes that damned him to hell for daring to stand up to her. On the other hand, what experiences had led her to expect always settling for second best? His curiosity prickled.

'But you enjoy a bit of drama,' he murmured quietly.

'No, I *don't*,' Vivi contradicted squarely. 'I particularly don't want to be arguing with you if we're going to be stuck together for the next few months. We're both adults. We can agree to differ and still be friends, can't we?'

'Friends and lovers? I can do that. Friends with benefits? I can do that too,' Raffaele traded softly. 'But I can't do platonic with you.'

Vivi settled wide shaken eyes on him, another issue that had not been discussed prior to their wedding cropping up to fill her with anxiety. 'Why not?'

'Because I want you and I don't intend to cheat on you and betray my marriage vows,' Raffaele replied succinctly. 'It's cards-on-the-table time, Vivi. There's no room now for games, lies or half-truths. If…as you put it…we're to be *stuck* together for the next few months, we might as well see if we can make a go of this marriage.'

Vivi dealt him a horrified appraisal. 'No…no, that's not what I want at all! That's not what I signed up for either!'

Shock was reverberating through Vivi. If they lived like a normal married couple, she would get close to him again and run the risk of losing her every defence. She wasn't capable of sharing a bed with him and then walking away with a cheery wave after their child was born. No, she would get attached, want *more*, start feeling as though he were hers. And he wouldn't be hers, he wouldn't really be hers in any way, not in a trial marriage that would only last a few months.

'Neither of us willingly signed up for any of this,' Raffaele parried. 'But this is our life now.'

'Don't talk about *our* life!' Vivi spat back at him in a passion of bemused fury. 'We won't be sharing anything, least of all a bed!'

Raffaele released his breath in a slow measured hiss, his classic profile taut, and said nothing.

His silence trundled like a concrete mixer in the back of her head, mocking her rage.

And, ironically, even his silence drove Vivi crazy! How could he drop a bombshell of that magnitude on her and then say nothing? He expected to share a bed with her? He expected her to consider making their marriage a *real* marriage? She was gobsmacked and furious that he had mentioned neither of those aspirations before the wedding. Too darned clever by half to show his hand early when she might still have withdrawn her consent, she reasoned bitterly.

'We've arrived,' Raffaele murmured softly, the liquid notes of his husky accent tugging on every nerve ending in her taut body.

Vivi stared out wide-eyed and panicked at the grand hotel where her grandfather had decided to hold the reception. She and Raffaele had argued fiercely all the way from the church to the hotel, she registered in horror. So much for being friends, so much for being reasonable! How could she be reasonable when she was dealing with an utterly unreasonable guy? She had never been a saint, had never been good at keeping her mouth closed when she should, had always preferred to speak her mind and take the consequences, but the consequences just kept on piling up with Raffaele!

Mustering what little remained of her composure, Vivi slid out of the limo, smiling when Zoe came running to help her protect her dress from harm. Immediately it occurred to her that, as Raffaele had suggested, she could bring Zoe out to Italy with her. For a split second she liked that idea, knowing she would find her kid sister's presence a great comfort, but what would it be like for Zoe? Zoe would loathe being plunged into the midst of the conflict between her sister and her husband. It would be cruel to involve her vulnerable sibling in such an explosive set-up.

Vivi put on her game face to greet the wedding guests. She noticed that her grandad was still wreathed in smiles and surmised that Winnie had not yet broken Vivi's news. Stam Fotakis didn't smile when his plans went awry. It finally dawned on her that leaving that unpleasant duty in her sister's hands was horribly selfish. Why should Winnie have to deal with the mess Vivi had made?

As Raffaele put a hand on her hip to urge her in the direction of the function room, Vivi broke free. 'I have to speak to Grandad,' she muttered in explanation.

'Won't it wait?' he asked.

''Fraid not,' she said flatly, approaching the older man to ask if there was anywhere that they could have a private word.

'What's up?' Stam asked, reading her anxious expression as he ushered her into a private lounge.

Vivi breathed in deep. 'You're not going to like what I have to say.'

'I often don't—since when has that bothered you?' the older man asked wryly.

'I won't be leaving Raffaele after the reception,' she told him stiffly. 'I'm pregnant and I've agreed to stay with him until our baby is born.'

Stam's dark eyes flashed with an icy glitter, his face turning set and distant. 'He *dishonoured* you.'

'No, I think it would be fairer to say that I dishonoured myself,' Vivi muttered, striving to hold her head high and not take refuge in any craven excuses. 'But what's done is done and at least I went through with the wedding so the baby will be born within wedlock. That sort of thing means a lot to Raffaele and I think it's important to you as well.'

'Mancini dishonoured you…and I warned him!' Stam ground out as if he hadn't heard a word she had said.

'Please don't start arguing with him, Grandad,' Vivi murmured ruefully. 'I'm a big girl and I'm equally to blame for this development.'

'He took advantage of your innocence,' her grandfather condemned in a bitter undertone.

Vivi swallowed hard with dismay and embarrassment. 'We'd better get back to the reception,' she pointed out hurriedly, seeing no point in lingering now she had got her confession out of the way.

Winnie arched a brow as she saw Vivi emerge from the room a step in front of the granite-faced older man. 'You told him?' she whispered.

'It wasn't fair to lumber you with it,' Vivi muttered apologetically. 'He's mad but he'll get over it.'

'As long as he doesn't take his ire out on your bridegroom,' Winnie groaned.

Vivi was speeding across the dance floor to the top table when Arianna intercepted her, her pretty face anxious. 'Do you think we can be friends again?' she pressed.

'I was never not friends with you,' Vivi pointed out.

'I listened to Raffaele and I shouldn't have…but, you know, he's almost always right about people…only for once he got it wrong and I got it right,' she completed with a rueful smile. 'I'm sorry, Vivi, that I didn't fight to keep our friendship alive.'

'That's all right. We all make mistakes,' Vivi said with greater warmth and forgiveness, her attention snatched back from the sight of her grim-faced grandfather glowering at Raffaele. 'But we can make a fresh start now that we're part of the same family.'

'We've got so much to catch up on,' Arianna trilled with anticipation. 'I can't wait to hear how you and my brother met up again. It must've been love at first sight for both of you.'

'Must've been,' Vivi slotted in diplomatically, watching her grandad stalk off and suspecting, by the stiff angle of Raffaele's proud dark head, that the encounter had left him equally angry.

'And then because Raffaele didn't tell me about you getting married until the last possible moment, you didn't even get a hen party!' Arianna lamented.

'Not much of a fan of them,' Vivi confided, reckoning that that omission was the least of her worries.

'Come and meet Tomas,' Arianna urged, closing an eager hand over Vivi's arm. 'We're getting married this summer.'

'Good grief...' Vivi said in surprise as Arianna practically dragged her in her enthusiasm across the room to meet a sandy-blond male of about Raffaele's age, who smiled cheerfully at her and closed a fond arm round the bubbly brunette by her side.

Vivi hastened back to the top table before anyone else could divert her. The hard stamp of tension on Raffaele's darkly good-looking face warned her that whatever her grandfather had said or done had caused offence and she blamed herself for that development entirely. After all, she was a grown woman and she had not gone into the situation with Raffaele blindfolded. She had known that her grandfather had a particularly old-fashioned outlook on young women and sex and instead of paying heed to that awareness she had blundered and failed to even cover her tracks. Now it looked as though Raffaele was expected to pay the price of her miscalculation and her grandfather's disappointment in her.

'What did Grandad say to you?' Vivi asked baldly.

'Nothing I'm prepared to repeat,' Raffaele breathed

with a raw, wrathful edge to his dark deep voice as he struggled for the first time in his life to rein back his temper.

Stam Fotakis was a cheat. Raffaele had kept his side of the bargain by marrying Vivi but Stam had refused to hand over the dossier on Arianna, arguing that Raffaele had dishonoured his granddaughter instead of treating her with respect.

All of a sudden life had become very complicated again, Raffaele acknowledged in seething frustration. He had *counted* on reclaiming that dossier once he had put that ring on Vivi's finger but, evidently, Fotakis now planned to continue holding that threat over his head for months to come. Raffaele had not been prepared for that development when he'd set up a sting calculated to deprive the older man of his overweening pride in his own financial acumen. He had not realised that Vivi's grandfather would still have the weapon of that dossier in his possession. He gritted his teeth. Well, it was too late now to change anything, and he would have to let the chips fall where they may…

'I'm sorry,' Vivi muttered ruefully.

'Why should you be sorry?' Raffaele fielded drily. 'You haven't done anything wrong. I was the one in the wrong.'

As the first course of the wedding breakfast was delivered, Vivi blinked. 'What on earth are you talking about?'

'I'm older, more experienced. I was reckless.'

'So was I, but don't make a meal of it,' Vivi advised ruefully. 'Grandad was born and raised in another age and he will always blame the man involved for anything of that nature. But we know different.'

'*Do we?*' Shimmering dark golden eyes fringed by spiky black lashes held hers fast and her chest tightened, her mouth running dry as a slightly dizzy sensation ran through her, blurring her clarity of thought.

'Yes, we do,' Vivi reasoned, fighting to reclaim her brain. 'I'm every bit as intelligent as you are and we were both equally irresponsible.'

'I hope you're not planning to tell our child that some day,' Raffaele quipped.

Vivi coloured. 'Hardly.'

Her grandfather stood up to give a short, pithy speech, forcing that uneasy dialogue to a close.

'I saw you smiling at Arianna. That was kind of you considering how your relationship ended,' Raffaele remarked warily over the main course.

'I always liked your sister and I'm quite sure that you bullied her into cutting off all communication with me,' Vivi admitted.

'I'm not a bully. At the time I thought I was being wise on her behalf and protecting her from a malign influence.'

'Well, you may not be a bully,' Vivi conceded reluctantly, 'but we both know that Arianna does exactly what you tell her to do. I can't hold that against her.'

'She was very attached to you. I had to be brutal,' Raffaele revealed grudgingly.

'I suppose you said a lot of unrepeatable stuff about me,' Vivi surmised grimly.

Raffaele bit out a groan. 'Let's not rehash the past.

I got it wrong and I've admitted it and now I'm apologising. Leave it there.'

Vivi breathed in deep and slow, wondering if she would ever be able to move past that old hurt. Why was she so sensitive where he was concerned? After all, looking back, nothing much had happened between them. She'd had a girly infatuation with him. He had kissed her, encouraged her, then misjudged her and walked away. Her own vulnerability galled her. A stronger woman, she told herself scornfully, would have long since forgotten so casual and short-lived an episode. But for Vivi, who had always fiercely guarded her heart from hurt and then mistakenly let down her barriers, a sense of pained humiliation still lingered like an old scar that hadn't quite healed.

'So, where do we go from here?' she muttered rather sourly.

'It's simple,' Raffaele asserted with characteristic confidence.

'It's anything *but* simple,' Vivi contradicted tartly.

'But it still all comes down to one baseline,' Raffaele intoned silkily. 'Either you want me…or you don't.'

And with that one challenging sentence, Raffaele cut through the argumentativeness that was usually Vivi's strongest defence and left her bereft of breath.

CHAPTER EIGHT

'BREATHE IN!' ZOE URGED.

'I *am* breathing in!' Vivi protested, fighting to get her breath back and giving up the struggle to flop back on the side of the bed, the striped cropped jeans she had planned to wear to leave the hotel still unzipped. 'What on earth is the matter with them? They were a perfect fit a couple of weeks ago!'

'That tight they'd be very uncomfortable to travel in,' Zoe pointed out gently.

Vivi gritted her teeth. 'I can't have put on that much extra weight already,' she argued. 'I'm only a few weeks pregnant.'

'Maybe you're one of those women who's going to blow up into a balloon straight away,' Zoe muttered uncertainly. 'You should ask Winnie. She knows more than me about being pregnant.'

'A balloon?' Vivi repeated, aghast. 'Thanks a bundle for that image, sis!'

'Well, how would I know what it's like?' Zoe pulled an apologetic face.

'What on earth am I going to wear?' Vivi snapped, standing up and peeling off the jeans in angry frustration. 'All my stuff was packed and sent over to Raffaele's town house, where I *thought* I'd be living, but it's now probably on its way to the airport.'

'I'll give you the skirt and top I was planning to change into this evening if I got too warm,' Zoe offered helpfully.

'The skirt'll be too short for me,' Vivi framed, tears suddenly stinging her eyes in a shocking surge. 'Oh, my goodness, what's the matter with me? I'm crying!'

'Pregnancy hormones…have you forgotten what Winnie was like? She could've wept the Thames dry while she was carrying Teddy! Emotionally, she was all over the place.'

Vivi resisted a ridiculous urge to throw herself down on the bed and sob over the jeans that didn't fit and the skirt that would be too short and breathed in deeply to get a grip on herself instead. She couldn't afford to be out of control around Raffaele and she didn't want to make a fool of herself either. A few minutes later she had donned Zoe's pencil skirt. She only just got the zip up, thanking heaven that her sister was a little curvier in shape. The lace top was a tad more revealing on her than it was on Zoe and a little too tight and short.

'I look awful!' she proclaimed. 'I'm showing far too much skin.'

'I doubt if Raffaele will complain,' Zoe teased. 'Your legs look fabulous.'

'Well, it's this or nudity.' Vivi sighed, averting her eyes from the very slight hint of a curve on her once concave stomach. Her body shouldn't be showing a change in shape so early, she thought irritably. Was she eating the wrong stuff? Was there a special pregnant lady diet she should be following? Was she bloating? That was probably all it was, she told herself soothingly. Didn't she have enough to worry about with Raffaele having thrown down that demeaning gauntlet of a challenge?

Either you want me...or you don't.

Talk about going back to basics! Of course, she wanted him on that most primitive level, and well did he know it! She had always wanted him *that* way. It wasn't something she was proud of but there it was, an instant chemical attraction that had yet to dim. Of course, being around him more, maybe familiarity would breed contempt, she thought hopefully as she emerged from the lift into the busy hotel foyer.

Winnie bustled over to her. 'Why are you wearing Zoe's clothes?'

'Don't ask,' Vivi said with a grimace. 'Where's Raffaele?'

'In the bar with a very beautiful blonde called Elisa,' Winnie responded with slightly raised brows. 'Apparently she's absolutely gasping to meet you and become your new best friend.'

'Really?' Vivi queried on a note of surprise.

'Feels it's her duty as Raffaele's "friend".' Winnie made air quotes with a roll of her eyes. 'To advise and support you.'

'Support me?' Vivi cut in.

'Since you're a fairly new arrival on Grandad's social scene and Raffaele's,' her sister clarified.

'Well, we'll see about that,' Vivi said dismissively, heading for the private bar attached to the function room, her cheeks colouring self-consciously because she was hyper-aware of her less than elegant appearance. What was cute and appropriate on Zoe's tiny frame looked rather different on her own tall, skinny body, she thought ruefully. And a tall skinny body developing curves where nature had never intended curves promised to be a nightmare to dress.

None of those thoughts crossed Raffaele's mind for a moment when he saw his bride walking towards him with the fluid grace of a dancer. She looked like a fantasy come to life, he thought with an almost adolescent knee-jerk reaction that shocked him. But there she was, gorgeous legs on display from her dainty ankles to her slender knees to her pale shapely thighs. The top hugged a swell of bosom that there seemed to be more of than he recalled, but reasoning over the why or the how of that was beyond Raffaele at that instant, fighting as he was not to display his arousal in his neat-fitting trousers. He gritted his teeth.

'Vivi…come and meet Elisa,' he urged, reaching for her hand to tug her closer.

Vivi shot him a glance, virtually allowing herself a five-second scrutiny, not allowing herself any longer and, bang, the effect of him hit her like a wave, drowning her in impressions she didn't want. But there he was, the luxuriant blue-black hair he kept short glimmering below the lights, his bronzed classic profile lightened by a smile, his beautiful mouth sculpted and sensual, and she wanted to flatten him to the carpet and taste that mouth and everything else about him right then and there because he was *stunning*. And stunning being the only word she could come up with unnerved her even more. It took effort to recover from that volatile instant of abstracted erotic imagery and deal with the woman being introduced to her.

'Elisa Andrelli.' The beautiful blonde air-kissed her on both cheeks but only by dint of stretching up on tip-toe. '*Dio mio*...you are tall!'

'Six feet in these heels,' Vivi agreed with a helpless grin. 'My sisters are both small. I loved it when I outgrew them, because Winnie was older but I could talk back to her more effectively when I could look *down* at her.'

'Always a fighter,' Raffaele remarked with amusement.

'You'd better believe it.' Vivi could feel the blonde's critical appraisal moving over her outfit and inwardly she cringed before lifting her chin with determined indifference.

'I know the best places to shop in Florence. I could advise you on what to wear for special occasions,' Elisa told her earnestly.

Vivi smiled. 'I don't need advice in that line but thanks, all the same,' she murmured with as much sincerity as she could fake.

Raffaele walked her away. 'That wasn't very generous of you. Elisa can come across as patronising, but she is well-intentioned.'

Resentment sent hot pink flying up into Vivi's cheeks. She was beginning to realise that she was much more thin-skinned around Raffaele than she was around other people. A hint of criticism from him and her blood boiled. But she should've known he would recognise her insincerity, only she hadn't expected him to chide her for it. 'And who *is* Elisa?'

'Our nearest neighbour. She has quite a sad history: she married her childhood sweetheart a few years ago and he died of leukaemia,' Raffaele told her. 'I think she's quite lonely. She was part of a couple from her teens and missed out on making female friends. Young beautiful widows aren't much in demand.'

'How unfortunate,' Vivi muttered, her face telegraphing her discomfiture as she resolved to make fewer snap judgements about the people she met. Suddenly she was very much aware that she had been willing to dislike another woman purely because she was attractive and appeared to know Raffaele well. Why was that? She was possessive of Raffaele, she acknowledged in dismay, as possessive as a dog guarding a bone.

Either you want me...or you don't.

Her face burned, her sense of vulnerability tightening every nerve in her slim body because she wasn't stupid enough to make the same mistake she had made before with Raffaele, contriving to get attached with very little encouragement and then left standing while *he* walked away. That demeaning image was stuck in her memory like a warning wake-up call. No, she didn't want him and she wasn't going to have anything more to do with him than she had to, she told herself angrily. She would act the wife in public if forced to do so but the play-acting would stop behind closed doors.

Raffaele studied his bride as she napped on his private jet. He stood up to drape a throw over her, wishing he had thought to mention the sleeping compartment where she would have been more comfortable. He needed to start thinking about such matters, he censured himself. Vivi was his wife, his responsibility, as was the child she carried. Bluish shadows were etched below her lowered lids and she looked pale. Of course, she always looked pale with that fair skin of hers but she was probably exhausted, and he hadn't yet even got around to organising medical support for her in Florence. *Sì,* he would definitely have to step up his game in the caring stakes. Poised there, he resolved to spend more time looking after her than thinking about bedding her.

Vivi woke sleepily when her shoulder was gently shaken and she blinked up at Raffaele and muttered drowsily, 'How long have I been asleep?'

'Since we took off. We've landed.'

Vivi's eyes widened and she stood up in haste, retrieving a shoe that had fallen off and smoothing down her rumpled clothing. 'Where to next?' she asked, trying not to sound weary of the journey when she had slept through most of it.

'A helicopter will drop us at the *palazzo* in twenty minutes and then you can relax,' Raffaele clarified smoothly.

'What's a *palazzo*?' she enquired.

'A large house. I was born at the Palazzo Mancini. It has always been my home,' he explained, taking her elbow to escort her down the steps and off the plane as if she couldn't be trusted to manage them safely on her own.

'Grandad lives in a large house outside Athens,' Vivi

told him while thinking about the much humbler accommodation that had been hers from childhood until Stamboulas Fotakis had entered the sisters' lives and tucked them into a very comfortable little town house he owned in London. 'I have very little memory of my parents. I was very young when they died and Zoe was only a baby. Winnie remembers them, though.'

'That's tough,' Raffaele conceded, engaged in working out the logistics of loading her into the helicopter in her high heels. Deciding simply to go for the obvious, he swung round to lift her bodily off her feet and settle her on board.

Thoroughly flustered by the arrival of a man in her life who could actually lift her as if she were a lightweight, Vivi settled down in the nearest seat and did up her belt. She didn't like the lurch as the craft took off and even less did she enjoy the flight as queasiness afflicted her empty stomach and Raffaele, like some sort of glorified Italian tour guide, endeavoured to point out famous landmarks to her when the last thing she wanted to do was be forced to look out of the windows at the sights.

'It's the *palazzo*…the best view of it you can have,' Raffaele persisted with all the sensitivity of a torturer as she fought mind over matter not to throw up. 'You're not looking…why are you not looking?'

'Because I'm feeling sick, you dummy!' Vivi hissed at him fierily.

His disconcertion almost comically palpable, he grabbed a receptacle for her and guilt assailed her because she didn't know why she was blaming him for her physical condition when she herself was equally responsible. 'Sorry,' she mumbled, hanging on for grim death to the receptacle and praying that she did not have to use it in front of him.

Mercifully, only a few minutes later, the helicopter settled back on solid earth again and she emerged from the craft with a sigh of relief but still feeling dizzy and sick.

'You should've told me you weren't feeling well.' Raffaele sighed, urging her towards the waiting car he had ordered when he himself usually walked.

'It's the first time it's happened and you said it was a short flight so I didn't want to make a fuss,' she responded truthfully. 'All the same, I shouldn't have bitten your head off the way I did.'

'I'm getting used to it,' Raffaele incised lazily. 'You often speak before you think…'

In other words, she was the only real dummy in the relationship, Vivi interpreted, feeling sorry for herself. Only at that point did she begin to notice the sheer immensity of the building they were heading towards. It was a giant stone property that stretched across an entire hilltop with windows that had a blinding sparkle because there were so many of them. '*This* is your home?'

'*Sì,*' Raffaele said fondly. 'The home of my family for centuries.'

No wonder he had said Zoe could move in with them if she liked, Vivi thought weakly, overpowered by the grandeur of the statuary adorning the façade and the formal gardens the car was traversing. Her impressions didn't improve when a stout little man in a formal suit,

introduced to her as Amedeo, ushered them into a huge
hall decorated with breathtaking frescoes and where a
uniformed staff line-up awaited them. Vivi felt overpowered by the splendour of her surroundings, fearing
that at any minute someone would call her an impos-
tor and ask her to leave because she did not belong in
such a place. She wasn't fancy enough, she ruminated
uncomfortably, certainly *not* fancy enough to have a
personal maid and a social secretary working full-time
to see to her needs, but nonetheless she was introduced
to an example of each.

Certainly, however, it was an education to see the
evident pomp and ceremony with which Raffaele lived
and which he quite took for granted, she surmised. After
all, if he had been born and bred to such a magnificent
home and a very large staff, it was normal for him, but
she was convinced that it would never, ever feel normal for her and that she would race back to her own life
when their marriage ended with nothing but a sense of
deep relief. No, she would have to have a rather difficult
conversation with Raffaele concerning his startlingly
unexpected suggestion that they spend the months of her
pregnancy seeing if they could make a go of their marriage. Raffaele needed a wife to *match* his *palazzo*, not
a one-time junior employee with a marketing degree,
not a young woman who had merely fallen accidentally
pregnant and whose sole claim to fame was a very rich,
eccentric, controlling and argumentative grandfather.

'Would you like to rest for a while?' Raffaele enquired as if she were a very elderly lady.

'No, I'd like a shower, a change of clothes and something to eat,' Vivi confided as they walked upstairs at a stately pace. 'You know, I'm not the slightest bit delicate, Raffaele… I'm just pregnant and a little more tired than normal.'

'You felt sick,' Raffaele broke in to remind her.

'Par for the course,' she parried carelessly, keen not to encourage him to view her as weak and in need of care and supervision.

'I don't know anything about pregnant women.'

'Why would you?' she traded as tall double doors were opened wide on a gigantic bedroom with a grand gilded four-poster bed on a platform as a centrepiece. 'Good grief, this place is like a museum. Is this one of the sights?'

'It's my bedroom,' Raffaele admitted, reckoning that he wasn't quite getting the reaction he had hoped for from his new bride. 'You're not into history, are you?'

'Not living in it, no,' Vivi admitted truthfully, wondering why she was being brought into his bedroom and then scolding herself for not appreciating that it was perfectly natural for a member of staff to show a new bride into what was presumably supposed to be the marital bedroom.

'You are free to do whatever you like with your own bedroom to make yourself more comfortable here,' Raffaele told her, crossing the room to cast open a communicating door that opened onto another door, and opening that as well.

She was to have her own bedroom, of course she was, she registered, following him to step through the double doorways and see another big bedroom, which was mercifully not quite as much of a museum piece as his. The bed was shaped like a swan but the décor was lighter and brighter and less rich and ornate. 'It's beautiful,' she said, because it was.

A quick smile flashed across Raffaele's lean, startlingly handsome face, lightening his eyes to the gold of a sunset fringed by black lace and, just looking at him, she felt her breath trapped in her throat for an instant.

'This room hasn't been occupied since my stepmother died, so I had it refurnished and decorated for you.'

'You really didn't ever think of us staying in London,' she acknowledged thoughtfully.

'No, this is very much home for me and I hope that in time it can feel like your home as well,' Raffaele asserted with impressive sincerity.

Impressive, Vivi tagged, because she couldn't credit that he could possibly mean such a sentiment when it came to her. After all, she was the wife he had taken merely to make a fat profit and he had originally intended to leave the church without her by his side. According to Raffaele, her pregnancy had changed everything, but it hadn't changed the essential facts, which were that he had never expected to stay married to her and that they were ill-suited as a couple, she reasoned briskly. All the wishing in the world couldn't alter those inescapable facts.

In the aftermath of that reflection, she marvelled at the hollow sensation of emptiness and sadness filling her, reckoning that she was still tired and feeling intimidated by her opulent surroundings. 'What time's dinner?' she enquired.

'Eight but I've ordered a snack for you. It'll be brought up soon.'

He had barely stepped back to his room when a knock on the door sounded and *her* maid, Sofi, appeared, holding a tray. Vivi tucked into the delicious omelette and salad and the lingering nausea ebbed. Sofi reappeared and eagerly showed her the built-in closets in the dressing room where her small collection of clothing huddled shamefacedly on opulent padded hangers and in scented drawers. Life at the *palazzo*, Vivi reckoned, was a complete other world, far removed from that of more ordinary folk. She sat down on the bed while thinking about that and somehow fell asleep again, waking with a start to see the light beyond the windows dimming and wondering what was wrong with her that she was feeling so incredibly tired all the time. And then she remembered…*again* and patted her tummy ruefully.

It was after seven and, recalling that dinner was at eight, she was galvanised into action, stripping where she stood to dive into the bathroom and straight into the shower. She would get her hair straightened again, she thought blissfully. She hadn't had time before the wedding with so much else to stress about. Now she could return to being sleek, straight-haired Vivi, whom she much preferred. She might be pregnant but that didn't mean she had to let her standards slip. She was unnerved to return to her bedroom, luckily wrapped in a towel, to find Sofi hovering expectantly to offer assistance. What with, Vivi wondered, until Sofi shyly confided in quite good English that she was trained to do different hairstyles and make-up.

Vivi sped into the dressing room and snatched her single long dress off a hanger, a gown bought for her first meeting with her grandad and hopefully formal enough to meet the *palazzo* standards. Sofi turned out to be a miracle with curly hair, leaving Vivi scrutinising her elegant reflection in surprise, for she had never been very good at putting her hair up and when she had, it had still always looked like an uncontrollable mop.

She picked her path delicately downstairs in her high heels and was ushered by Amedeo into a grand salon, where she took one glance of consternation at Raffaele and realised that she had got it wrong. He sported faded jeans and an open-necked white shirt. He looked fantastic but the difference between them sent colour surging into her cheeks. 'This really says it all about us,' she commented, indicating her long dress, her attempt at formality, with a dismissive hand. 'You dressed *down* and I dressed *up*.'

'What does it say about us?' Raffaele pressed. 'I simply assumed that after a long day in formal clothing you would prefer to relax…as do I.'

'But you normally dress up for dinner, don't you?' Vivi cut in, determined to make her point even if it was beginning to feel like a petty point.

'*Sì*,' Raffaele conceded grudgingly.

Vivi lifted her chin, mortified colour lying in bright bars across her triangular face as she walked down to the foot of the room, keen to put as much space as possible between them. 'You don't need to dress *down* for my benefit, then,' she sniped.

Raffaele resisted the urge to heave a sigh and wonder

why he always, *always* got it wrong with Vivi. He tried to be sensitive and he embarrassed her. He tried to be caring and she got sick as a dog. 'I'm getting tired of your defeatist, negative attitude,' he intoned with complete honesty. 'I appreciate that you're in a situation not of your choosing, but I am as well and at least I'm trying to make the best of it.'

Caught utterly unprepared by that raw condemnation, Vivi coloured to the roots of her hair. 'That's not true,' she said stiffly.

'It is true. You misread everything I do. You hold spite. You judge me.'

'For living like a prince in a palace?' Vivi shot back at him defensively.

'I was born here…this is my life. You expect me to *apologise* for it?' Raffaele shouted down the length of the room at her, the sound of his raised voice cracking like a stinging whiplash through her because in her experience Raffaele *never* raised his voice and it thoroughly unnerved her. Out of the corner of her eye she noted Amedeo hurriedly retreating from the doorway and, if possible, she felt even more humiliated.

'I've had enough of this,' Vivi told him, throwing back her slight shoulders and stalking back towards the hall.

Raffaele planted himself in her path like an immoveable rock. 'No, for once in your life, you're going to listen to me.'

'Like hell I am!' Vivi snapped back at him like a spitting cat. 'The day I listen to you while you talk down to me there'll be two blue moons in the sky and a flying pig!'

'*Listen* to me,' Raffaele ground out wrathfully, struggling to get a hold on a temper that he never usually lost.

Vivi told him very rudely where he could go and what he could do with himself when he got there and raced past him at the speed of a lemming ready to throw herself off a cliff. She climbed the stairs even faster, sped into her bedroom and just stood there breathing fast. Behind her the door opened and she spun round, as rigid as a stick of rock.

'We can do better than this,' Raffaele breathed in a driven undertone. 'I'm sorry that I shouted at you but sometimes you push me too far.'

'I have a habit of doing that with you,' Vivi muttered, somewhat mollified by the apology and relieved he no longer seemed angry. 'I don't know why.'

'Don't you?' Raffaele questioned, an eloquent ebony brow lifting, unimpressed. 'You do it to keep me at a distance.'

Vivi was appalled that he could interpret her behaviour that easily, that he had picked up on her need to avoid any form of intimacy developing between them. 'It's safer that way,' she mumbled in disconcertion.

'Not now that we're married with a baby on the way, it's not!' Raffaele countered scathingly. 'There's enough attraction between us to light a bonfire.'

Vivi stiffened even more. 'Speak for yourself,' she parried.

Raffaele had never met such a stubborn woman and he crossed the room to stand in front of her, only then noticing the tiny, almost imperceptible tremors shaking through her slender body; only then reading the anxiety in her wide eyes as the fear it genuinely was. 'Vivi… I would never ever hurt or harm a hair on your head,' he muttered shakily, so unnerved was he by the sight of a woman regarding him with fear.

'It was just…er…when you shouted,' she whispered, not sure she was even telling him the truth at that moment. 'I'm sort of programmed to run when men shout because when I was a kid it usually got violent and if you didn't get out of the way you got hurt!'

'I swear I'll never shout again,' Raffaele framed, lifting a not quite steady hand to smooth soothing fingers down the side of her flawless face to her soft, full pink mouth. 'Ever. I had no idea that was your experience.'

'It's not something you share freely,' she admitted brokenly, all shaken up by both the conversation and the manner in which their argument had gone downstairs. He had accused her of holding spite and judging him, constantly throwing up barriers between them, and she felt overwhelmed by the awareness that Raffaele was correct on every count. He had read her, she conceded guiltily, and called her bluff, refusing to allow her to continue hiding behind such empty excuses, and *that* had proved an utterly unnerving experience for Vivi. That was what had really sent her fleeing into retreat, she acknowledged in mortification.

'But if it's a trigger, it's something I should know about you,' Raffaele breathed, a long forefinger tracing her full, soft lower lip, the ever-ready pulse at his groin throbbing with helpless arousal. 'Believe me, Vivi… *dannazione*, I have many flaws but you will *always* be safe with me.'

And the rigidity went out of her taut length as if he had punched a release button and she smiled tentatively up at him. 'Sorry about the drama…and Amedeo heard you shouting and he looked *so* shocked.'

Raffaele's lean, darkly mesmerising features slashed into a reluctant grin. 'He's never heard me shout before. I'm very even-tempered.'

'Until you met me…'

'Until I met you, *bella mia*,' Raffaele husked, lowering his proud dark head.

And she knew he was about to kiss her and she told herself to step away but inexplicably she stayed right where she was, heat curling up in her pelvis at even the thought of that much contact.

CHAPTER NINE

RAFFAELE'S MOUTH CAME down on hers with the most earth-shattering sensuality she had ever experienced. It was everything her charged body needed even though she refused to admit that to herself. Desire shot through her as hot as the bonfire he had mentioned, her breasts swelling, her nipples tightening hard, her core growing slick and damp. All just from a kiss! She argued with herself while pushing instinctively into the hard, muscular heat of him. She wanted so much more, craved the most primitive of possessions, was completely shocked by the tide of sexual longing he could awaken in her.

'Per l'amor di Dio... I ache for you,' Raffaele husked thickly, tugging at the spaghetti straps of her dress and dragging the bodice down to reveal the pink pouting buds of her breasts while stalking her backwards, down onto the swan bed. He closed his mouth hungrily to a tantalising peak, dimly registering that he was aroused beyond belief and questioning the reality because sex had never done that to him before. Unfortunately for him, however, he was getting a real high out of it, so he repressed that nagging flare of dismay and ignored it.

'I love your breasts,' he growled.

Vivi lay back on the bed, belatedly disconcerted by what she was allowing to happen between them. She was being shimmied out of her dress by determined hands and she wasn't doing anything to stop him.

I don't want to stop him. The words stood out like some sort of brain Morse code she couldn't ignore. Her fingers speared into his black cropped hair and she trembled, seduced by the lashing of his tongue and the nip of his teeth over her achingly sensitive breasts. She wanted more, she wanted so much more, not least the irksome ache at the heart of her sated. She was just using him for sex. That was all right, wasn't it? Nothing scary about that, was there? Men had been using women for sex for centuries, so, there was no reason why it couldn't occasionally be done the other way round, she told herself, pulling him up to her to claim his passionate mouth for her own.

Heavens, his kisses were addictive, she acknowledged helplessly, lifting her hips to facilitate the removal of her last garment, barely crediting what she was doing, but she couldn't get enough of his mouth or the taste of him. And then there was the wonderfully solid weight and feel of him over her and the wickedly familiar scent of him, clean, musky man overlaid with a hint of sexy cologne. There was just something about Raffaele that got to her every time he got close. Her hands roved down his spine to his slim hips and back up again, tugging at his shirt when it got in her way. She found the buttons, doggedly released them, began to pull and he got the message, rearing up half over her to pull it off and throw it aside, looming over her to expose a mouth-watering display of well-toned pecs and abs.

Below those elegant suits he wore, he was all sleek bronzed flesh and lean, hard muscle. She loved his body, she realised, really, *really* loved his body, and that alien thought shook her into opening her eyes and blinking up at him.

'*Che cosa*...what?' he husked, staring down at her with stormy, dark golden eyes and lashes longer than her own.

'Nothing.' Not fair to bless a man with those lashes, she had thought the very first time she saw him. But his eyes were absolutely beautiful, his lean, dark features equally so. Raffaele hadn't been standing behind any door when the gifts were handed out at birth. Her heart was banging inside her chest like a drum tattoo and when his hand roved across her inner thigh, her body sang in a chorus of anticipation that was as terrifying as it was thrilling. He stroked her, lightly, almost play-fully, and her back arched and her hips rose, the hunger rising as demandingly as any bone-deep craving. And that was what it was, she conceded in a daze, a hunger so instinctive she couldn't fight it, couldn't control it, certainly couldn't snuff it out and go back to the inno-cence that had once been hers.

'If there's something bothering you, you should tell me,' Raffaele muttered, gazing down at her, enthralled by the pleasure of Vivi not fighting him for once, while, at the same time, suspiciously wondering what had brought about this miraculous change.

Vivi half slid out from under him to turn on her side and aimed her reddened lips at his. 'You're talking too much, taking too long,' she complained, because no way was she ever going to tell him the truth: that sometimes he mesmerised her into being a woman she despised, a weak woman, a woman without proper self-discipline and strength.

'No, tonight will be what our first time *should* have been but wasn't,' Raffaele declared with maddening resolve.

'It was good…us…the first time,' Vivi protested through compressed lips.

'Good, but crazy and brief—like a couple of teenagers having sex for the first time,' Raffaele reasoned, his pride clearly troubled by that reality.

'You will just never do what I ask you to do!' Vivi complained helplessly.

'Probably not,' Raffaele agreed smoothly, amusement gleaming in his dark eyes as he crushed her ripe pink mouth under his again, taking the easy way out of the disagreement. It went against the grain with him to accept that he had gone utterly out of control the first time he had been with her and in retrospect that performance shamed him. This time around nothing short of an earthquake was going to be allowed to distract him.

His hand massaged over a long smooth thigh, relishing the satiny feel of her skin and the receptive dampness at her core even more. He wanted to do something he hadn't done before because he wanted to drive her wild. It momentarily crossed his mind that in the past he had been a fairly selfish lover, accustomed to the women in his bed doing everything possible to please him. It had never been the other way round for Raffaele. He had never been eager to impress a woman with the gratification he could give her and the novelty of that challenged and aroused him.

As Raffaele lowered his tousled dark head in the direction of the most intimate part of her, Vivi froze. 'No, I don't want that!' she gasped, hot with embarrassment at the very thought of it.

Vivi closed her eyes, telling herself she could get through anything and that presumably he would know what he was doing. That was one advantage of an experienced lover, she told herself even as every nerve cell in her body rose up in anger at the very idea of Raffaele being with another woman. Seriously, what was that reaction about? she asked herself in bewilderment. She didn't own him. Theirs was a temporary marriage of convenience and once their baby was *born*…

A sudden burst of intense pleasure blurred her active brain and a startled gasp was wrenched from her. In the compelling timeless moments that followed, crashing waves of sensation gripped her slender length, building and building to a peak of rapture that was spellbinding. Her hips rose and the heat in her pelvis mushroomed up to grip her entire body. A tiny shriek escaped her and she saw stars as the tension broke and she reached a breathtaking climax. Raffaele grinned down at her and crushed her mouth under his as the after quakes of pleasure still cocooned her. Her arms came up and locked to him, some need in her responding to that urge to hold him close and unnerving her.

'You're amazing, *tesoro mio*,' Raffaele growled, sliding her thighs back, moving over her.

Nobody had ever called Vivi amazing before and her eyes literally prickled with tears, tears of gratification that shook her. But before she could even think about that, Raffaele was hauling her legs round his waist and sinking into her with delicious force. It felt exquisite, it felt like everything she had been waiting for as her body expanded to take him, and the glorious friction of his every movement took her by storm. Her heart raced and she could feel his movement and it felt like the most intense bond ever. Little ripples of pleasure gathered again at her core and she gasped for breath, her body rising and falling against his, exhilaration shooting through her in wave after wave as he plunged deeper into her, inflaming every sense. Vivi was sensually enthralled as the sweet tension began to gather and tighten in her pelvis again, her excitement climbing, all control wrested from her as he ravished her with pleasure. Another orgasm rocked her like a blazing star igniting inside her pelvis, paroxysms of liquid hot delight sending radiant tendrils though her entire being. She cried out, feeling him shudder over her, the locked-tight tension of his lean, strong body as he too reached the same peak and it broke over him.

Sliding free of her, Raffaele disconcerted Vivi by tugging her back into him and closing both arms round her. 'As we've just demonstrated,' he intoned, 'giving this marriage a chance can work.'

And that fast, Vivi was shot from the blissful aftermath of relaxation to wanting to pound both her fists into Raffaele, because she could hear the smile in his voice and couldn't bring herself to look up and actually see that smile. When had she decided to forget what Raffaele was really like? He *always* had an agenda and he had just used sex to entrap her in an arrangement she had already refused to consider.

She should've had more control, should've said no, should've looked beyond the moment, she told herself with self-loathing. Only she never managed to do any of those sensible things when Raffaele was involved, did she? He always caught her unprepared because he was calculating, clever, usually working towards a goal.

'It was just sex,' she muttered uncomfortably. 'Meaningless.'

Raffaele gritted his teeth on an angry response. 'It's not meaningless because you're my wife. This is a beginning,' he informed her arrogantly.

'But I didn't agree to trying to stay married,' Vivi almost whispered, because having that conversation while lying naked in bed with him felt very *very* uncomfortable. 'I think that's silly. We agreed to stay married until the baby's born and surely that's enough.'

Raffaele shifted position and lifted up to gaze down at her. 'What have you got to *lose*, Vivi? Whatever happens, we'll be together for the next few months,' he pointed out levelly. 'If it works, it works, if it doesn't, it doesn't.'

'It's never going to work between us,' Vivi assured him.

Shimmering dark golden eyes held her evasive gaze

fast. 'But you could at least give us a chance…it's not going to cost you anything to *try*.'

Vivi lost colour and closed her eyes tight against the intrusion of his. He made trying sound so reasonable, was making her feel bad for refusing. But then he didn't know, couldn't possibly understand that she was trying to protect herself from getting hurt. Just suppose it worked for her but not for him? Where would that leave her? Just suppose Raffaele was being a manipulative nasty guy? This was, after all, a man who had been willing to go to quite extraordinary lengths purely to marry her and make a profit even though he already appeared to be wealthy beyond avarice. Wasn't it entirely possible that Raffaele felt that if he had to be stuck with a wife for the next six months and more, it might as well be a wife who also shared his bed? Wasn't it possible that he was only trying to use *her*?

Or was that her paranoia talking? Raffaele had to have many more sophisticated options than her available if all he wanted was sex, she reasoned more calmly. Even though he was now ostensibly married, there would still be willing women on offer because he was rich and young and very, very good-looking. Also, incredible in bed, she added and felt her face burn. So why would he want to simply use her for that physical outlet? No, she finally decided, the odds were that Raffaele was serious when he suggested giving their marriage of convenience the chance to become something more real. And if Raffaele was making a genuine offer, cowardice—the fear of being hurt—wasn't a good enough excuse for her to employ as a defence.

Vivi breathed in deep and opened her eyes, colliding with his intent dark golden stare. 'Everything in this household is way over the top—too fancy for me,' she admitted uncomfortably.

'You can make changes,' Raffaele said easily, startling her with that immediate response. 'The *palazzo* hasn't had a proper mistress since my mother died over twenty years ago and it's running on the same lines now as it ran under my grandmother. Nothing has been altered.'

'Arianna's mother didn't change anything?' she asked in surprise.

'She was always too busy chasing her next high or she was in rehab or she was shopping,' Raffaele said drily.

'You really didn't like your stepmother.'

'There was nothing to like. She had no interest in the man she married, his son or even her own daughter. She wanted the money, the lifestyle, nothing else. I remember her screaming at my father that Arianna was a dreadful accident.'

Vivi grimaced and said nothing, registering, however, that Raffaele's rich, privileged childhood had not been as idyllic as she had naively assumed. If he had made false assumptions about her, she acknowledged ruefully, she had been equally guilty of making similar assumptions about him based on superficialities like wealth and background.

'Why didn't he divorce her if she was so awful?'

'He believed marriage was for ever, but I also suspect that he couldn't bring himself to face the fact that he'd made a hideous mistake remarrying so quickly after my mother's death. He was lonely, still grieving, not in the right state of mind to make such a major decision. I don't think he even appreciated that women as corrupt as Arianna's mother existed in the world. He'd married young, he couldn't have been very experienced with women.'

'So, I could make changes here if I wanted to?' Vivi recapped.

'Of course, it's your new home. If you're going to raise our family here, it has to be comfortable for you.'

'Don't put the cart in front of the horse,' Vivi urged stiffly. 'Sometimes, you are so pushy, Raffaele.'

'And sometimes, you *like* that about me,' Raffaele fielded, bending down to claim her parted lips with his, sending a dizzy spurt of pleasure travelling through her slender length.

Vivi rolled out of reach, not trusting him that close, not trusting herself either. 'We may not work. We don't have much in common.'

'Incredible chemistry and a baby are a healthy start,' Raffaele informed her with a sizzling smile.

'All right, I'll give it a go,' Vivi told him grudgingly, sliding off the side of the bed at speed when he tried to reach for her again. 'I'm going for a shower and then I want to eat. I'm ravenous.'

'My foster mum was a darling but her husband was a drunk,' Vivi volunteered ruefully. 'And there were horrible violent scenes when he came home at night and he would beat her up. I'd be at the top of the stairs listening to him shout, praying he wouldn't hurt her too much. And then one night he came into my room and sat down on my bed and told me I was a big girl...'

'What age were you?' Raffaele cut in rawly, incensed by what she had experienced while she was still a child.

'Thirteen, not very developed either,' she muttered with a shudder. 'He tried to touch me and I screamed and his wife came in and, well, that was the end of that placement.'

'I hope the next placement was happier for you,' Raffaele breathed through gritted teeth, shocked against his will by what he was learning about the care system for orphaned kids.

He had also learned that the stepmother whom he had loathed had not been quite the nightmare he had believed her to be, certainly not when compared to some of the parenting figures Vivi had endured. His stepmother's essential lack of interest in him and his father's care had protected him from the worst of the older woman's drug excesses. Separated from her sisters, however, because it was hard to find a single home willing to take all three girls, Vivi had been deprived of the family support she had relied on as a child.

'That was the worst that ever happened to me and, to be honest, it wasn't so bad. Zoe had it roughest of all of us. That's why she is the way she is,' Vivi told him ruefully, suddenly feeling uncomfortable because as a rule she was very private when it came to her childhood experiences. 'How on earth did we get talking about this stuff?'

Raffaele hid a smile because he had learned how to

draw Vivi out of her shell and he wasn't about to share his secrets. Ironically it was new to him to wonder what made another human being tick. Beyond the business world where sizing up opponents was the norm, Raffaele never got close enough to people to care why they did what they did or why they thought a certain way. To date, Arianna was the sole exception to that rule and now Vivi was the second, and both of them were family, which put them in a different category, he reasoned. If only it were as easy to get Vivi to take his advice, actually listen to him, he conceded with considerably less assurance, because Vivi was as stubborn as a rock planted in concrete.

Over the past seven weeks, his bride had begun to look more noticeably pregnant, something which she complained about because apparently her sister had not shown the same signs at such an early stage. In addition, Vivi was as sick as a dog several times a day, something which she simply took in her stride and brushed off as an unalterable fact of pregnancy. She had yet to go near a doctor, had an innately practical attitude to her condition and saw no need for medical intervention. Raffaele had learned to hide his concern because she did, *literally*, consider her pregnancy to be none of his *male* business, but he had contrived one small achievement by persuading her to go for a scan that afternoon with a top-flight obstetrician in Florence. Luckily for him, Vivi wanted to see their baby and was willing to take advantage of that facility.

Feeling somnolent even in the shade, Vivi contemplated her rising stomach above her bikini pants with disfavour. She *was* blowing up like a balloon, just as Zoe had forecast, and there was nothing she could do about it. Vivi refused to let pregnancy get in her way of making the most of her enjoyable new life.

Enjoyable? She smiled at that disconcerting acknowledgement, gazing out at the beautiful sun-drenched gardens surrounding the private pool. The view beyond was of even more spectacular countryside, composed of rolling hills and vineyards and olive and orange orchards and, as far as the eye could see, it was all Mancini land. Slowly she had begun to understand that Raffaele lived like a feudal prince because his family had once been feudal rulers. His father had used his ducal title throughout his life but Raffaele didn't use his, respecting that the Italian Republic no longer legally recognised the titles of the former nobility. Only the fact he didn't use the title didn't stop the staff routinely referring to him as Il Duca or to herself as La Duchessa, nor did it change the outlook of the many people who revered Raffaele for his pedigreed heritage. It no longer surprised her that Raffaele had that aristocratic cool and dignity that had once set her teeth on edge.

It was the weekend, which meant that Raffaele was at home, and she loved the weekends best when she generally had him all to herself. Possessive...*much*? Oh, yes, very possessive, she conceded ruefully. He ticked every box in the husband stakes, as if he had contrived to swallow some magic potion that endowed him with perfection. No such thing as a perfect man, her hind brain reminded her, but if there had been, Raffaele would top the lists. Initially she had been shocked by how considerate he could be of her comfort.

She had changed stuff at the *palazzo*, stuff that had been set in stone for probably at least a hundred years, she thought wryly. They no longer ate in a giant dining room surrounded by staff. Now they dined in much more relaxed surroundings in a much smaller room. The menus had also become considerably less elaborate because they were both quite sparing eaters. She had banished dated practices like the staff lining up to greet Raffaele every time he came home and he hadn't even noticed their absence. Piece by piece she was dragging daily life at the Palazzo Mancini into the modern world.

The biggest challenge, however, had initially been her need to find something to occupy herself while Raffaele was at the bank. She had been amazed to discover that the *palazzo* was opened to the public one day every week, a day when Raffaele had been routinely in the habit of removing himself to the family apartment in Florence for twenty-four hours. Although a very private man, Raffaele saw it as his bounden duty to open his ancestral home to tourists, and to architectural historians and interested conservationists. At the same time, Vivi had stayed home one week simply to see the entire process in operation and she had been appalled at the mess that was being made of the experience, with untrained staff struggling to cope with questions they couldn't answer and poor Amedeo giving a very boring talk about the family.

Vivi had taken over by engaging a young historian to write up the Mancini family history and then hiring proper tour guides. She had plans for a shop and a café as well for the end of the tour because there was so much unused space in the *palazzo*. Those plans had kept her very busy. Surprisingly, Raffaele was content to allow her a completely free hand but worried that she was taking on too much of a burden, until it finally dawned on him that Vivi adored being busy and needed a purpose in life as much as he did.

Yes, she took time out to shop with Elisa and Arianna, both of whom she got on with very well. They had dined several evenings with Tomas and Arianna, who occupied a very smart house in Florence. Zoe had come for a visit and had shared their grandad's marital plans for her with remarkably little concern, insisting that she would easily cope with living abroad in a palace as a princess for a few months, which was evidently all that was to be required of her. Winnie and Eros had stayed as well for a weekend, Winnie confiding that she had not suffered nausea anything like as badly as Vivi was.

Viv's fingers spread fondly over her stomach as she wondered if she was carrying a little girl, having read somewhere the possibility that a female baby could increase morning sickness in a mother-to-be.

'You're drifting off to sleep,' Raffaele murmured, long brown fingers stroking the back of her hand. 'Let's go in. You need to get ready to go for your scan.'

Vivi lifted her head and collided with sunlit dark golden eyes, and a spasm of pure lust that made her feel wanton gripped her. Almost every time she looked at Raffaele, she wanted him with an instinctive hunger she couldn't suppress. He was fantastic in bed, that was all it was, she told herself; it was perfectly normal to crave pleasure. They shared his museum piece of a bed every night, for it was a lot more comfortable than it looked and she was as guilty of luxuriating in his body as he was in hers. Just good clean fun—well, maybe not quite clean, she conceded, thinking of some of the stuff they did, her mind drifting drowsily over X-rated imagery that once would have shocked her. And the most amazing thing about Raffaele, she thought wonderingly as he tugged her off the sunlounger, was that, in spite of that conservative, conventional vibe he put out so strongly, he was wildly and wonderfully uninhibited in bed.

'You're miles away…what are you thinking about?'

Her cheeks warm, Vivi grinned at him as he tugged her up the rear staircase that led to their rooms.

'*Seriously?*' Raffaele stressed, reading her expressive face, arousal pulsing through him instantaneously. 'If this is what being pregnant does to you, *bella mia*… I hope you appreciate that I'm likely to want to *keep* you pregnant.'

'No, not with the sickness and all the rest of it. You get one child off me and that's your lot!' Vivi laughed.

As she melted into the heat of him in the privacy of their bedroom, Raffaele recognised the joy that Vivi brought into his life and marvelled at that startling revelation, for it was not a sensation he had recognised or even expected to find since leaving childhood behind.

The obstetrician watched the screen as the nurse worked the wand over Vivi's exposed stomach. Standing up, she addressed the nurse and the wand lingered while Raffaele's hand tightened on Vivi's, sending alarm kicking up through her. Was something wrong with her pregnancy? Had something worrying been spotted?

The older woman smiled down at Vivi's anxious face and indicated the screen. 'I can tell you that you have one healthy boy here and behind him his twin, who may or may not be another boy. We can't get a good enough view yet to tell the second child's gender.'

'*Second* child?' Vivi gasped in alarm. 'You mean… there're two of them?'

'Twins,' Raffaele confirmed not quite steadily. 'We are going to be the parents of twins. Dr Fanetti suspects that that is what is causing your extreme nausea and may also explain why your pregnancy appears to be developing faster than normal.'

The rushing fast pulse of their babies' heartbeats filled the room and, blinking, Vivi rested her head back in shock. Twins. *Two* babies. The very concept silenced her when adjusting to the prospect of even one baby had demanded so much from her.

'This is really exciting news,' Raffaele intoned. 'We have never had twins in the family.'

'A twin pregnancy is riskier,' Vivi reminded him nervously, because she had listened to the obstetrician's strictures, which warned that she had to be more careful carrying twins than she would've had to be with a singleton pregnancy. She would grow larger, get more tired and there was a greater chance of premature birth. 'I'm stunned. Two children, not one, that's a massive jump from having no children at all.'

'We'll have a *team* of nannies,' Raffaele assured her soothingly. 'You will have extra check-ups, more frequent scans and tests. Every possible precaution will be exercised on your behalf.'

Vivi was thinking that she could never ever have managed two babies alone and was belatedly grateful that she had agreed to give their marriage a fair chance. And it was working brilliantly, wasn't it? Her heart was touched by his unashamed excitement about their children. How could she look past that? Any woman would value that in the father of her kids. *Kids?* Raffaele was so supportive and she hadn't expected that from him, in truth hadn't expected many of the things he had done. She got flowers all the time, she got gifts, was now the proud owner of several valuable and very beautiful pieces of jewellery. She was beginning to understand why Arianna adored her big brother and marvelled that she had misjudged him to such an extent when he had misjudged her two years earlier.

In retrospect the speed with which he had reached that misjudgement still surprised Vivi, because Raffaele was usually a much more controlled and cautious individual, yet he had leapt in to make positively clumsy wrong assumptions about her.

'We could go out tonight to celebrate,' Raffaele murmured, grabbing her hand and bringing it to his lips to press a kiss there, his beautiful eyes locked to her with undeniable appreciation.

'Well, look at you,' Vivi teased. 'One child was a shock and *two* is a—'

'A miracle,' Raffaele slotted in cheerfully.

'You really do like children.'

Raffaele grinned, pure masculine charisma in the sunlight. 'If they're ours, a mix of us both...*sì*.'

Vivi only just resisted the urge to stop in the middle of the street and kiss him. She wasn't the demonstrative type, never had been, but sometimes there was something about Raffaele that made her want to hurl herself into his arms like a homing pigeon. Oh, go on, she urged herself, why not admit it? She was besotted with him because he made her so happy, made her feel beautiful, irresistible and special. Two years back she had been on track to falling for him for all the most superficial reasons: his looks, his sophistication, his charm. Two years on she looked for more from a man and Raffaele delivered on every front. She wasn't ashamed of loving him. In fact, loving Raffaele made her feel whole, as if she had come full circle from the youthful insecurities that had frightened her off getting too attached to anyone beyond the safe circle of the sisters she trusted.

As they climbed out of the limo outside the *palazzo*, Amedeo came hurrying out to address his employer in a flood of Italian. Raffaele glanced across the lawn to where a large helicopter was parked, the pilot standing beside it. 'Your grandfather's here.'

Her brows rose. 'Oh...that's unexpected.'

Raffaele expelled his breath in a slow hiss. 'And he's probably in a rage, so let me handle him.'

'Why would he be in a rage?' Vivi asked blankly.

'Actions I took as payback for something he did to me but, now he's in the family, we're rather stuck with each other and it wasn't the brightest idea... I admit,'

Raffaele admitted tautly. 'You go upstairs and I'll deal with him.'

'No, he's my grandad and a shocking old grouch,' Vivi countered. 'I'm not leaving you alone to deal with him.'

Raffaele grimaced. 'Vivi…there's stuff you don't know and this is not the moment for you to find out. Stay out of this…*please*.'

In shock at that admission, Vivi fell back a step, her tense face pale below her mop of curls. She still hadn't had those curls straightened, she acknowledged absently as the giant mirrors in the hall threw back a myriad reflections of her hurrying figure. Why not? She hated her curls but Raffaele adored them, genuinely adored them, was forever trailing his fingers through them, rearranging them and admiring them.

But what didn't she know? What did Raffaele not want her to find out? She hovered outside the grand salon they rarely used and even through the solid wooden door she could hear the roar of Stamboulas Fotakis shouting about losing millions of pounds. Millions of pounds? How was that possible? And what could Raffaele possibly have to do with that loss? Taking a deep breath, Vivi opened the door and walked in…

CHAPTER TEN

'TELL ME WHAT's happening here,' Vivi urged, stalking deeper into the room, a tall slender figure in a turquoise sundress that floated round her long shapely legs. Both men turned to look at her.

Stam Fotakis was flushed and furious. 'I've lost millions of pounds thanks to your husband! He set a trap for me.'

'A trap that wouldn't have worked had you not been tracking my every move in the financial markets and buying where I bought,' Raffaele pointed out levelly.

'Why would you track what Raffaele does?' Vivi pressed her grandfather.

'He's a financial genius, Vivi. I'm not the only one doing it,' the older man growled angrily. 'But this time he laid a false trail and I bought into it and now I've lost a pile of money.'

'Explain,' Vivi told Raffaele, her soft mouth tightly compressed.

'I showed interest in a company that I knew was about to go bust and, now that it has, Stam is blaming me for his reverses,' Raffaele countered tautly.

'And you did it to him deliberately,' Vivi registered in shock at her husband's behaviour, visibly paling.

'It was nothing more than a slap on the wrist,' Raffaele ground out in exasperated dismissal. 'Stam may be howling as though he is mortally wounded but what he's lost is a drop in the bucket in comparison to his wealth.'

Vivi continued to stare at her husband in bemusement. 'But why would you do that? Why wouldn't you warn him? I get that he shouldn't be spying on what you do but, if you knew it was happening, why weren't you just blunt with him? Why would you want him to lose money?'

'Leave it, Vivi,' Stam said abruptly, guessing where the dialogue could be heading and deciding to back off rather than expose a secret that would do him no credit in his grandchild's eyes. 'What's done is done.'

'No, you don't get to come storming in here shouting without explaining yourself,' Vivi interrupted, her violet eyes flaring off the older man to rest instead on the younger. 'And you don't get to do what you appear to have done to my grandad without explaining why.'

Raffaele stalked across the room, all flaring energy and anger, swinging back to face her from the window, his lean dark features hard and grim. 'I was…eventually planning to tell you but at the start of all this I didn't trust you with secrets that could damage my sister.'

'Arianna?' Vivi queried, more confused than ever, but gutted by his declaration of distrust even if she was struggling not to betray the fact. 'What the heck does Arianna have to do with any of this?'

Raffaele compressed his lips. 'Stam compiled a

very harmful dossier on Arianna's biggest mistakes in life and threatened to release the information to the media. The dossier contains embarrassing revelations that would enrage her fiancé's very old-fashioned family. I was afraid that publication of that dossier would destroy her future with Tomas.'

Vivi was appalled by what she was hearing. 'But why would you do such a thing?' she began asking Stam in horror, but even as she spoke the picture was falling into place and making a dreadful kind of sense. 'You *blackmailed* Raffaele into marrying me! *Both* of you lied to me! *Both* of you allowed me to believe that it was some kind of business deal. How could you threaten Arianna like that, Grandad? She never did anything to harm me…'

Raffaele watched in amazement as Stam Fotakis lowered his head in shame, his eyes evading the younger woman's. 'It was the only lever I had with Raffaele, Vivi. He had to pay for the damage he had done to your good name and I had to have a means of pressure to use. I didn't relish that means but I was prepared to *use* it, for your sake.'

'*My* sake?' she whispered sickly, a shudder of revulsion and denial racking her slender frame. 'You blackmailed Raffaele by threatening his sister's future. That's disgusting and unpardonable. Where is this dossier now? Destroyed, I hope.'

'Not yet. I was to receive it at the wedding but Stam refused to part with it,' Raffaele broke in harshly. 'He was planning to continue holding it over my head and I couldn't live with that option.'

'You broke the terms of our deal!' her grandfather barked angrily. 'Vivi is pregnant.'

'You forced us together again. You can carry the can for that!' Raffaele slammed back rawly at the older man. 'And now you've hurt Vivi, which I can't forgive.'

Vivi parted bloodless lips because sheer shock at what was unfolding was making her feel a little sick and dizzy. 'You've *both* hurt and disappointed me.'

The terms of our deal?

The phrase rhymed over and over again in her head as she left the room and headed for the stairs. Her marriage was a deal, the cruellest of deals. How had she ever contrived to forget that reality? But she *had* forgotten, had buried the awareness deep that Raffaele was supposedly marrying her to make a fat financial profit. Although, knowing what she did about his character, that explanation had never made much sense to her, she had still accepted it and questioned it no further. Really, when she had buried her head in the sand to such an extent, it was her own fault that she was now being slapped in the face by the unsavoury truth.

Raffaele had been *blackmailed* into marrying her, forced to gain her agreement to marry him by the threat to Arianna's future. She knew how much Raffaele loved his kid sister and knew there was little he would not do to protect her from harm. She was also aware from some of the things that Arianna had told her in the past that her sister-in-law had made mistakes she regretted. For goodness' sake, who hadn't done that? But Arianna was a wealthy and beautiful heiress and what she did was less likely to go unremarked.

Looking back, Vivi could see how she had wilfully misinterpreted Raffaele's behaviour before their marriage. In her mind she had somehow contrived to view his very persistence in seeking her agreement to marry him as a backhanded compliment related to her attraction. Without even thinking about it, she had also freely forgiven Raffaele for attempting to use blackmail on her by threatening redundancies at Hacketts Tech.

In the end that concern had been wiped out by the much more personal fact that she was pregnant and that was why she had married him. She had, however, allowed nothing to get in the way of her developing feelings for Raffaele, the love she had denied even to herself for so long. On a deep-down level she had always wanted Raffaele and, having finally got him, she hadn't asked too many awkward questions about what had first brought him back into her life.

The terms of our deal.

That was the foundation of the marriage she was so happy in, not exactly a solid basis for a relationship in which to raise children, she conceded, stricken. As she sat down on the foot of the bed, she felt like a rag doll that had been shaken so hard its stuffing was about to fall out. As a wave of nausea assailed her, she raced for the bathroom. Afterwards, she hung onto the marble vanity unit to stay upright and freshened up with trembling hands. Feeling physically weak and sick only made her feel worse because she was seeing how she had lied to herself all along, trying to conserve her pride by refusing to admit how much she loved Raffaele even when it was painfully obvious.

How much worse was it to be forced to accept that, even though she had believed she and Raffaele had grown close, the guy she loved, the father of her twin babies, still hadn't trusted her enough to share the truth with her? The unfortunate fact was that *he* was the real *victim* here. No, that reality wouldn't have sat well with Raffaele's fierce pride. Indeed, being forced to do anything would go against the grain for Raffaele, but he had still sacrificed his pride for his sister's sake. And why did that make her love him *more* when she ought to hate him for all of it? In despair, Vivi pressed cooling hands to her tear-streaked cheeks, struggling to hold in the intensity of her warring feelings.

The bedroom door opened without warning and framed Raffaele's tall dark silhouette in the doorway. 'Stam's gone. He's going to return the dossier to me and then I'll destroy it and hopefully that will be the end of that,' he breathed in a raw undertone. 'Thank you for that.'

Vivi's eyes looked bruised against her pallor, her vivid hair making the contrast all the more striking. In that moment, she looked so frail and vulnerable he wanted to scoop her up and wrap her in cotton wool to protect her. But, sadly, he couldn't protect her from the fallout of his own mistakes and his sins had truly come home to roost now, he acknowledged unhappily.

'Why are you thanking me for anything?'

'Stam was ashamed to have you know what he had done and he doesn't want anything more to do with that threat,' Raffaele clarified wryly.

'Does Arianna know about this business?' Vivi demanded.

'Nothing about any of it,' Raffaele admitted. 'She would've been devastated and it wouldn't have been fair. I should've looked after her more carefully when she was younger and ensured that she didn't get into situations she couldn't cope with. That she *did* is on me.'

'In our marriage you were the victim but you let me go on thinking that *I* was,' Vivi muttered tightly. 'You never even hinted that you were being…constrained. You may not believe it but if you'd told me what Grandad was doing I would have intervened.'

'At the beginning I didn't trust you. I still harboured all those wrong convictions about you,' Raffaele reminded her ruefully. 'Arianna had ditched you as a friend. Why was I going to assume that you would be sympathetic in any way towards her?'

'Yes, I can see why you thought that…*at the beginning*,' Vivi stressed tightly. 'Were you ever planning to tell me the truth?'

Raffaele flinched, black lashes lowering over stunning dark eyes, his sculpted mouth compressing into a strong line. 'Probably not,' he conceded, disconcerting her with that unexpected admission. 'I knew it would upset you and I didn't want to upset you. You learning that I was blackmailed to the altar wasn't going to materially change anything between us.'

'I deserved the truth whether it would have upset me or not,' Vivi pointed out. 'It was unfair to keep me in the dark.'

'Initially I agreed to marry you because of the dossier on Arianna,' Raffaele framed tautly. 'But long before we got to the church I had a whole host of other reasons for marrying you.'

'Only *one* reason… I was pregnant,' Vivi reminded him resolutely.

'Reason *two*, I couldn't keep my hands off you. Three, you light up my world in the weirdest way. Four, I screwed up two years ago with you and lost you and I wasn't about to risk losing you again.'

Her smooth brow furrowed. A little colour was returning to her drawn cheeks. 'Screwed up…*how*?'

'I met the girl of my dreams and I was falling for you and then all that brothel stuff came out in the newspapers and I reacted violently. I assumed I'd been an idiot with you. I hadn't been that attracted to anyone before and I felt foolish. I jumped to conclusions without examining the evidence. I walked away when I should've had the courage to trust my own instincts and *stay*.'

'You were falling in love with me?' Vivi almost whispered, so shaken was she by what she was hearing. 'Two years ago?'

Raffaele jerked down his chin in a silent nod of confirmation and tears sprang to her eyes and overflowed. 'That scandal cost us so much.'

'*Sì*…' Raffaele agreed, crouching down at her feet and seizing both of her hands in the strong grip of his. 'Which is why I was perfectly happy for Stam's blackmail to remain a dirty little secret for ever. What's a little blackmail in the family circle when I get to be with the woman I love? And I *do* love you… I love you so much I don't have the words to express it, *amata mia*.'

'You love me?' she mumbled unsteadily.

'I'm afraid so. I'm absolutely devoted to you and I'm never letting you go,' Raffaele asserted, rising upright and gently tugging on her hands to raise her too. 'I was in trouble the minute I saw you again but I didn't have to think about it because I was panicking about the dossier on Arianna. I knew I had a serious problem when I stole your virginity on a sofa, which is the very reverse of cool. All the same I knew it was love when I was happy that you were carrying my baby. I've never felt this way before. I didn't think I even had it in me to feel emotions like this,' he confessed with intense dark golden eyes locked to her appreciatively. 'Together you and that love have turned my world upside down.'

'Have we?' she asked breathlessly, wrapping two possessive arms round him and holding him close, revelling in the heat and strength of him.

'I'm much more flexible now. I've abandoned my clockwork routine that I used to hate having disrupted,' he admitted with an irreverent grin. 'I'm late getting into the bank in the morning because I stay home until my wife is awake and so I can make love to her again… you are *not* an early riser, *cara mia*. I leave the office early when I miss you. I've even come back for lunch a few times. I used to be a workaholic, a bit of a joyless character, to be frank. That's why I told you that you light up my world, because it was the truth that it was rather dark and boring before you came into it.'

'I just had no idea you felt this way about me,' she whispered in a joyful daze.

'Where have your wits been? I stick to you like white

on rice. I rarely leave you alone. All I want is to make you happy...to make up for all the unhappy times you went through before I was around,' he intoned with a raw emotional edge to that declaration. 'I love you with the sort of intensity I didn't believe I even possessed.'

'I love you too...and two years ago I was falling for you as well,' Vivi confided, suddenly feeling remarkably generous towards him. 'When you walked away you hurt me and that's why I tried to keep you at a distance this time around. I thought I needed to protect myself.'

Raffaele ran soothing fingertips down the side of her face. 'I'm sorry I hurt you but, if it's any consolation, I was hurt as well, which was why I reacted so badly back then. This time I didn't want to risk anything going wrong, so I *buried* the blackmail story.'

'You still should've told me,' Vivi warned him. 'A wife is supposed to be for good *and* bad times.'

'I know. I told Stam he was a terrific matchmaker, which, ironically, infuriated him. I mean, Winnie and Eros are mad about each other. I could see that at our wedding. And now, here we are, another well-matched pair.'

'But we're not well matched on paper!' Vivi protested. 'I still don't know *how* we work.'

'It's our special magic, *amata mia*, and I, for one, am very grateful for it.' Raffaele claimed her anxious mouth with a passionate kiss that left her breathless and her desire to understand the mystery of their happiness receded along with it. 'Talk later?'

'Is this you trying to bargain again?'

'It's called negotiation,' Raffaele assured her loftily

with amusement dancing in his gorgeous eyes. 'And I will have you know that I am very, *very* good at it.'

Vivi laughed and yanked his tie to draw him down to her on the bed, where she had arranged herself invitingly. 'I'm good at other stuff...'

'I know,' Raffaele agreed fondly as she dragged off his jacket, disposed of his tie and embarked impatiently on his shirt buttons, love and desire combining to drive her on with wild impatience. 'I love the way you strip me whenever you take the notion. I'm all yours.'

Vivi gave him plenty to love in the following hour, matching his passion with every fibre of her own, and excitement flamed over them because all worry had been forgotten and their intimacy had a sweeter edge after the truths they had shared. Afterwards, lying in his arms, thinking of all the many signs of love he had shown her and she had stubbornly refused to recognise, Vivi finally trusted enough to let happiness bubble through her and she contemplated her starry future.

EPILOGUE

EIGHTEEN MONTHS LATER, Vivi sat with her sister, Winnie, while she fed her second child, a little sister for Teddy called Cassia. Cassia was adorable with her dark curls but not quite as adorable, in Vivi's opinion, as her own much-adored twins, now aged one, very lively little boys crawling about the floor and getting involved in all sorts of mischief.

Matteo and Andrea had been born a little earlier than their due date, and by Caesarean section, but had been perfectly healthy, if a little heavy for their mother's slender frame. The pregnancy had been more testing than the delivery and had entailed bed rest in the third trimester when Vivi had developed crippling back and hip pain. That aside, Vivi was really enjoying motherhood and was giving Arianna, already going through her first pregnancy after her wedding the previous year, all the support she could. Slowly but surely her previous friendship with Raffaele's younger sister had revived, although she was probably closer to their near neighbour, Elisa.

Her sisters were regular visitors and possibly the biggest surprise of the past year had been Zoe's transformation into a woman to be reckoned with. Certainly, Vivi thought fondly, none of them could have forecast that development, but it was a very welcome one because their youngest sibling was no longer a source of anxiety and concern for either Winnie or Vivi.

In addition, much of the resentment their grandfather had fostered by insisting they marry men of his choosing had since drained away, vastly improving their relationship with the older man. Vivi, however, was still pretty cool towards Stam Fotakis because, although she had magically contrived to forgive Raffaele for those threatened redundancies because she knew he had been desperate to save Arianna from that dossier being made public, she was less forgiving of the way Raffaele had been treated by her grandfather. Eros had won an island and knowledge of his son's existence in marrying Winnie, Raffaele had simply been brutally blackmailed.

The older man was, however, still invited to all the main family get-togethers the sisters enjoyed because he did have one saving grace in that he totally loved his great-grandchildren and relished being a part of their lives. He could always be depended on to turn up with loads of age-inappropriate presents for the little ones in the family circle. Vivi's twins were the proud possessors of a fabulous train set that they wouldn't be allowed to play with until they were much older. But Stam did now try to fit in and behave like a family member and Vivi liked him the better on that score. Winnie was closest to the older man and Zoe had no quarrel with him whatsoever because in the end, as events had transpired, he had not had the chance to pressure Zoe into doing anything he wished.

Vivi was incredibly busy in her role as wife and mother. Her dressing room was now packed with clothes for wearing to regular social events and on the domestic front, since the one-day-a-week opening of the *palazzo* had grown into an enterprise and that was entirely her department, she was even busier. She loved having help constantly on hand with her sons because that freed her to organise the tourist arrangements at the *palazzo*. She had also been invited to play a role in a children's charity that Raffaele's mother had once been involved with. As Vivi loved to be challenged, the busier she was, the happier she was.

Winnie settled her infant daughter into one of the cots in the interlinking rooms that acted as a nursery suite at the *palazzo* and, smiling at the nanny hovering to look after the three children, accompanied Vivi downstairs.

'Do you think Zoe will make it this weekend?' Winnie asked hopefully.

'We'll have to wait and see. You know how pressured her schedule is,' Vivi murmured, her steps quickening on the stairs as she saw Raffaele stride into the hall and smile up at her.

When she saw him, her heart lifted—every time— and she felt light as air, as if nothing and nobody could ever hurt her again. It was a wonderfully grounding way for Vivi to feel after years and years of insecurity and distrust. It made her recall the therapy Zoe had gone through some years earlier and reckon that, perhaps, she could have done with some treatment as well, only she and Winnie had been so busy trying to 'fix' Zoe that neither of them had looked at their own childhood vulnerabilities.

Raffaele stood talking to her sister but his attention continued to stray back to his wife. Eros strode in from the pool and the two men exchanged news before the couples parted to get ready for dinner. Raffaele went straight upstairs to see his sons and Matteo and Andrea chortled with baby excitement and made a beeline for their father, who always provided fun. Vivi watched him scoop up the twins together with the affection that came so easily to him now. It had surprised her to see how much of a hands-on father her husband was willing to be, joining in bath times and play times with relaxed enjoyment. His own father had never unbent to such a degree with him, he had confided ruefully, but, as he had also pointed out, times had changed and his father had been raised with a great deal of formality by the staff and had rarely mixed with his parents when he was little.

One step inside their bedroom, Raffaele pulled her boldly into his arms and husked, 'You look ravishing today, *amata mia…*'

Vivi was already sliding out of her green cotton skirt and top, as hungry for his attention as he was for hers. In that line they had always been a perfect match for each other, she thought fondly. She lifted her slender hands to his face, fingers brushing appreciatively through the faint shadow of black stubble outlining his stubborn, passionate mouth. 'I always think you look gorgeous,' she told him truthfully, watching the colour darken his exotic cheekbones with secret amusement because he was never comfortable with any reference to his film-star looks. 'But what I love most about you is that you're *all* mine.'

'And you're so vocal about it, *bella mia*,' Raffaele growled with appreciation as he stalked her backwards and down onto the bed. 'As possessive as I am.'

'Match made in heaven,' Vivi whispered happily, looking up at him as he stripped with helpful alacrity.

'Or, as Stam would have it…possibly hell,' Raffaele countered with a half-smile, for he had a prickly relationship with the older man, who could never quite forget that Raffaele had dared to strike back at him for his blackmail.

'Heaven,' Vivi insisted with all the wonderful confidence his love had contrived to give her since their marriage.

'I love you,' Raffaele groaned after claiming a passionate kiss.

Vivi beamed up at him with a sunny smile, her violet eyes bright. 'I love you even more.'

'Competitive…much?' Raffaele laughed and silence fell as two very well-matched personalities proved all over again how very happy they could make each other.

* * * * *

MILLS & BOON

Coming next month

CLAIMED FOR THE SHEIKH'S SHOCK SON
Carol Marinelli

Khalid had kept his word, Aubrey realised. It had been dinner, that was all.

Except she didn't want it to be all.

It was Aubrey who wanted more and, despite what he thought her to be, it was everything else that he was—strong, sensual—that somehow made her feel safe.

Some day in the future Aubrey would know her first, and it was something she had silently dreaded.

Until now.

He could never imagine the wrestle that took place in her as they walked past the bar. Khalid could not know she was a virgin and how new this all felt to her.

All he responded to was the sensual air that surrounded them. 'I'll let the desk know now and then you can call for the driver whenever you are ready. Or,' he added, for he could resist her no more, 'you can come back to my suite.'

Aubrey stopped walking and as the sun returned to the night sky, she turned to face Khalid. Aubrey had never so completely met another's gaze before. If anything, she did her level best not to catch men's eyes, yet she held his, totally.

She saw the flecks of gold and the dark rim that seemed to hold inside it a circle of fire and he neither looked nor backed away from his invitation.

'I'd like that,' Aubrey said, for it was the truth. She wanted to be with Khalid, even if just for a night. She wanted him to be her first, yet he considered her way more experienced than she was. And if she told him her truth? Aubrey was rather certain that Khalid would politely wish her goodnight.

And so she lied by omission and chose not to tell Khalid her truth, and as he moved in to kiss her, his eyes still did not look away. Aubrey could feel the warmth of his mouth even before their lips had met and both closed their eyes as they did, for there could be no other way to sample such exquisite bliss. He kissed her so lightly that if she opened her eyes Aubrey was scared that he might have disappeared. That he might be a dream. Yet his lips pressed a little more firmly and parted hers.

Aubrey had truly never known a kiss, but even with nothing to compare it to she knew that his kiss was pure bliss. She could not have fathomed how, with such a gentle touch, her heart might tumble. It was as if he had found the weak spot within, the fracture line that, correctly tapped, might shatter her.

And he felt it too.

Tonight Khalid did not want the meaningless sex he survived on. He wanted to touch and to feel and for one night to fully indulge that. Today had been exceptionally hard—new grief and the resurgence of old grief had combined—but now there was a sweet reprieve and Audrey was the one he had found it with. She had consumed him on sight and it was a relief to finally hold her in his arms and kiss her lips as he wanted to.

But then he removed his kiss, and his hands held her hips as he made sure that Aubrey was clear as to the nature of his invitation.

'You understand that you won't be sleeping in the guest room?'

Oh, she did. Her lips ached for his and Khalid's hands on her hips were necessary for they held hers slightly back and prevented them from melding into his, as they felt inclined to do, and so she answered him honestly. 'I do.'

'Then come to bed.'

Continue reading
CLAIMED FOR THE SHEIKH'S SHOCK SON
Carol Marinelli

Available next month
www.millsandboon.co.uk

COMING SOON!

We really hope you enjoyed reading this book. If you're looking for more romance, be sure to head to the shops when new books are available on

Thursday 4th April

To see which titles are coming soon, please visit
millsandboon.co.uk/nextmonth

LET'S TALK
Romance

For exclusive extracts, competitions
and special offers, find us online:

- facebook.com/millsandboon
- @MillsandBoon
- @MillsandBoonUK

Get in touch on 01413 063232

For all the latest titles coming soon, visit
millsandboon.co.uk/nextmonth